DEATH PAINTS A PICTURE

THE PENELOPE STANDING MYSTERIES
BOOK 5

TESS BAYTREE

ONE

Penelope bounced on her toes, eager to keep moving along the sidewalk. Next to her, Brutus took an extra deep sniff of the rosebush.

"If you poke your eye out, you're on your own," she warned. It was a lie and the mastiff knew it. Brutus flicked an ear and kept sniffing.

The benefit of having lived over fifty years and having raised a child was the ability to both see and accept potential dangers, such as rose thorns near a mastiff's eye. Brutus hadn't injured himself all the *other* times he'd shoved his oversized nose into the depths of a thorny bush; there was no reason to think he would now.

Other benefits of aging had skipped past Penelope. Her curiosity still led her into awkward situations on a regular basis, she ate funnel cake at the county fair every year despite knowing how much she would regret it later, and even though she *knew* Esther was manipulating her, she still couldn't resist the mystery of the other woman's texted instructions.

Penelope didn't feel *too* bad about that last bit. Esther

had been a kindergarten teacher until she'd retired. Anyone who could pass out scissors to dozens of small children and keep them from cutting off each other's hair had magical powers.

Are you free 5-7? I'll explain when you get here. Bring Brutus.

It was that last part that piqued Penelope's curiosity. Esther often invited her along on outings to restaurant openings, funerals, and Rose Garden Society meetings. But Brutus would be welcome at none of those places. And whatever was going on, it wasn't happening inside Esther's house. The mastiff had a healthy fear of cats; Esther had six of them. The last time Penelope had taken her dog inside Esther's house, even a steady stream of treats hadn't been enough to keep him from standing with his head pressed against the front door.

Now, standing and waiting for the dog to finish sniffing... the suspense was killing her.

Brutus finally maneuvered his bulk so he could lift his leg and leave a few drops on one particular leaf. When all four legs were back on the ground, he consented to amble forward two steps before stopping at the next rosebush.

Penelope eyed the line of plants lining the sidewalk and calculated how much distance they had to cover. It was time for bribery. She held out the hand further from the roses. "Brutus, touch!"

The mastiff backed out of the rosebush with gratifying speed, then leaned past her to press his nose to her outstretched fingers.

"Good job." Penelope gave him a treat and walked forward briskly. She switched the leash to the opposite hand and extended her free hand in front of her. "Touch!"

The *touch* command was a useful trick for the times

when she needed to redirect Brutus's attention toward her, instead of a barking dog or someone delivering a package. It was also helpful when she noticed food on the ground before he got to it, but that happened so rarely, it didn't really count — Brutus's nose worked faster than her middle-aged eyes. In this case, Brutus was quite happy to give up on his leisurely sniff-and-stroll pace now that treats were involved.

A block later, they found Esther waiting in her wheelchair in front of her house. "Right on time! Let's go." She pushed the lever forward, and her chair sped along the sidewalk.

Penelope jogged to catch up, letting Brutus pull her along. The mastiff loved Esther, and not just because she slipped him food every time she saw him. Dogs responded to that kindergarten teacher's energy just like children. "Where are we going?" As Penelope came closer, she saw the drawing paper and baggie with charcoal stowed on Esther's lap. "The drawing class?"

When the town had unexpectedly received a grant funding an artist-in-residence program, the Rose Garden Society had chosen the candidate least likely to cause controversy, settling on a French man whose whimsical paintings were hanging in galleries around the world. Esther had fought for a Vietnamese woman who quilted diaspora scenes, but the fiber artist had been deemed "too political".

Penelope hadn't officially met the chosen artist yet. But the house Jean-Philippe Blanchet and his assistant were staying in had been a source of constant drama, making the inaugural year of the artist-in-residence program a complete success.

To fulfill the requirements of the program, Jean-

Philippe had to teach one class for beginners and one class for advanced students. Esther had joined the advanced class, which was life drawing using charcoal. Penelope, whose drawings had been known to inspire spirited debate of the *animal-vegetable-mineral?* variety in onlookers, had *tried* to sign up for the beginners' class. Esther claimed the class had reached capacity quickly.

Jogging on a manicured lawn, Penelope watched Esther's face. "Did you lose so many people in class that you need extra students or something?"

It wouldn't be the first time she'd been included in an event for the sole purpose of filling a seat. Most recently, she'd sat through a hilarious forty-five-minute reading from a detective novel by a local author for Esther's book club. Another member, Joyce, had accidentally invited noir novelist John Del Sol instead of celebrity chef John D. Sol and had been too polite to rescind the invitation. The other members of the group had read the novel's sample online and suddenly remembered longstanding prior engagements.

So Esther had bribed Penelope and Jake with dinner and a bottle of very good wine to ensure she and Joyce wouldn't be the only two people present. The novel had been terrible and highly inaccurate — even Penelope knew that, and *she* hadn't had a career in law enforcement like Jake had. But watching Jake trying to keep a straight face while John Del Sol spoke about his extensive research had been far more entertaining than she'd had any right to expect. And the author himself had been good company when he'd stopped talking about his book.

Esther halted her wheelchair long enough to look up at Penelope and laugh. "We might get away with that in an abstract art class, but life drawing? No." She shook her head and moved forward again. "Tara had an emergency and..."

The noise of a passing car drowned out the end of the sentence, but Penelope thought she heard the word *model.*

Shocked by the idea, Penelope stood where she was, staring after the speeding wheelchair. Model for a life drawing class? Really?

She'd never been naked in front of strangers since that one time twenty years before when someone had walked off with her clothes and towel at the campground while she'd been in the shower. Not that she had anything against nudity, per se. But these wouldn't be random strangers. These would be people she saw regularly.

Ahead, Esther slowed as she noticed Penelope had fallen behind.

Penelope distracted Brutus from his examination of a fence and they jogged forward again. Could she do this? It was rather flattering that Esther just assumed she would have no qualms about getting naked in front of ten people she knew. Still... "Isn't Roddy in the class? This might make having him bag my groceries awkward."

Frowning up at her in confusion, Esther asked, "Why would having Roddy draw your dog make things awkward?"

Oh.

Of *course.* They were going to draw *Brutus.* That's why Esther's text had told her to bring him along. Penelope exhaled in relief.

Meanwhile, Esther's expression cycled from confusion through understanding to mirth as she figured out why Penelope had been reluctant. She laughed, her head dropping back. "Oh, my dear, you are the *last* person I would have model. Sitting motionless for twenty minutes? You'd be lucky to make it twenty *seconds.*"

Esther had a point. Penelope stared down at Brutus. Now that he'd had a walk, the mastiff could be relied upon to fall asleep quickly and stay that way for at least an hour. Plus, he was already naked. "And Jean-Philippe is okay with this?"

"No idea." They began moving forward again at a comfortable walking pace. "If he isn't, we'll have to cancel class. There isn't time to get all the releases signed and notarized for another model, even if we had one. So it's either Brutus or we draw the cupcakes I baked for the after-class snack." She caught Penelope's glance at her cupcake-free lap. "I took them over earlier and locked them in the art supplies room before chair volleyball."

"Very wise." They stopped at the corner and waited for the light to change. "What's Jean-Philippe like?" Penelope had delivered mail to the house where the artist was staying, but his packages had been a prosaic mix of art supplies and cartons of American snack food. For some reason, Penelope had assumed a famous French artist would receive exotic cheeses and wine, not chips and salsa, but maybe those had been for his assistant.

"Both too French and not French enough to be real, but a decent teacher." At Penelope's quizzical look, Esther explained. "Toes have been the bane of my existence for thirty years, and he showed me a neat little trick that helped. But for all his accent... what Parisian drinks *smoothies*? And he doesn't smoke. I refuse to believe it."

The light turned green. "So you're saying he's too healthy to be French."

"No. Well..." Esther aimed her chair at the ramp going up to the sidewalk on the other side of the street and sped up. The last time crews had dug up the utility lines, they had tamped down the replacement asphalt by hand, leading to a gap waiting to trap anything with wheels. Penelope followed behind, ready to steady the chair if needed, but

Esther clattered up onto the sidewalk without incident. "Maybe. I'm just saying I wouldn't be surprised if he was hiding his past. But if you decide to look into his background, wait until the end of the residency. I'd still like to get his input on knees."

Penelope admired Esther's practicality as they went up the ramp toward the library. "I promise I won't aim Jake in his direction until you have the lower leg complete." Her husband's private detective business might be small, but she had no doubt he could get the dirt on smoothie-drinking, non-smoking Jean-Philippe in a matter of minutes.

Not that Jake would investigate someone without a reason — he was currently juggling three clients, looking for a missing uncle, painting, and doll, respectively. The uncle had vanished with funds from the family business, the painting hadn't been seen since the clients had moved into assisted living ten years ago, and the doll was a hideous thing that Penelope thought had likely been thrown away or destroyed, though it was worth more than Jake's car.

Roses perfumed the air around the building. Constructed in the decade the town was founded, the library had a grand air, with two stories overlooking a central courtyard and surrounded by a large rose garden. As the library's offerings had changed over the years and much of the catalog went online, the reference books had been consolidated to one half of the second floor, and the rest of the space given over to meeting rooms and teaching space. Every few years, the town council suggested erecting a newer, more easily maintained building in another section of town — which would, purely coincidentally, free up a large plot of prime real estate for development — but the Rose Garden Society had too much influence for the idea to move beyond quiet whispers.

Esther stabbed the elevator call button.

With a series of hisses and clanks, the cab appeared. It was an ancient hydraulic lift that had worked without fail nearly as long as Penelope had been alive. The door had an accordion grate that had to be manually opened, and the cab took nearly a minute to inch its way up to the second floor, but Penelope expected it would keep going for another decade or two. Which was good because the library didn't have any funds in the budget to replace it.

When Penelope opened the grate, Brutus eyed the elevator car suspiciously, but as soon as Esther rolled inside, he walked in and sat beside her. Only then did Penelope think to check the weight limit.

"We're fine," Esther said, interrupting her calculations. "This carries carts full of books all the time. And if we do get stuck," she added with a glint in her eye, "you might get a chance to go through the hatch in the ceiling."

Penelope closed the grate and hit the button for the second floor. The elevator shuddered, then began its slow ascent. Brutus leaned against her leg. Looking at the ceiling, Penelope saw only a grid of lights. "How do you know it has a hatch up there?"

"I don't. I just wanted to get moving." Esther narrowed her eyes. "We're nowhere near the weight limit, but if you thought about it too long, you would have taken the stairs and someone might have kicked you out for bringing a dog into the building. We really need a model for class." She lifted her chin. "Besides, if we get there early enough, I can get Jean-Philippe's help on some things before Joann shows up and monopolizes his attention."

Penelope kept her face straight with an effort. Joann would try the patience of a saint, which, admittedly, neither Penelope nor Esther was. She had only herself to blame for the spectacle that had been her daughter's wedding, though Joann didn't see it that way.

The elevator bumped to a stop, and they exited. After the cramped confines of the ancient elevator, the library interior was a spacious wash of light, with daylight streaming in from the special UV-blocking windows facing the exterior and the courtyard. The only reference librarian in sight was helping a patron; she didn't see Brutus pad down the hallway toward the art room. The sweet smell of decaying books made Penelope sneeze.

Nobody else waited outside the closed door to the art room. "Looks like we made it here before Joann. Hopefully, you'll have the chance to learn how to draw beautiful knees today." Then Penelope considered Brutus's legs. "Or maybe not. Dog knees are really different."

Esther ignored that and leaned past her to open the door. "Bon jour, Jean-Philippe," she called out as she went inside.

Scents of clay, oil paints, and charcoal dust hung in the air. Ten easels had been placed in a loose circle around a rough wooden box in the room's center. Penelope shivered, thinking of splinters. Then she thought about how impossible the wood surface would be to disinfect and shivered again. Not that it would matter to Brutus, who regularly rolled in the most disgusting things produced by nature, but still. No wonder the life model had called in sick.

Esther glanced at her. "It gets covered with a blanket that we wash every week."

"I didn't say anything."

After claiming her spot by dint of setting her sketchbook down on an easel, Esther raised her voice to call toward the back of the room, where a closed door led to the supply closet. "Jean-Philippe?"

Penelope wandered the perimeter of the room, examining the abandoned sketches and paintings that littered every flat surface on the low bookcases lining the walls. To her untrained eye, they ran the gamut from something a child — or Penelope herself — could do, all the way to things that might hang in a museum. Next to her, Brutus sniffed the floor, fascinated by the olfactory art of the room. "Maybe he's late?"

"No. That's his bag over there. He must be somewhere else in the library, or —" Esther abandoned her easel. "The cupcakes are out. Do you have hold of Brutus?"

"Yes." Penelope tightened her grip on the leash. It was a sign of the quality of the smells in the room that he hadn't made a beeline toward the food. Brutus glanced up at her, then licked a spot on the tiles.

Esther picked up the plastic container from the paint-splattered table shoved against the wall. "Let me put them back in the supply closet so they won't distract him."

"Good move." Penelope crouched to stare at a clay creation that looked like a cross between a horse and a cow. "Maybe I could take a sculpting class."

"And sit still long enough to do all the detailed work? Chainsaw sculpture might be more your style."

Picturing that, Penelope smiled. It really *would* be more her style. She'd have to remember to bring it up to Jake when she got home. "They probably don't offer those classes at the library, though. Might be a little loud."

The sound of plastic and cupcakes hitting the floor interrupted her reverie. "Penelope!"

Penelope ran across the room, Brutus trailing behind her. At the entrance to the supply closet, she halted, taking in the scene.

Over the years, the closet had become the epitome of

the maxim "if you build shelves, stuff will fill them." Abandoned brushes, canvases, dried-up paints... Someone had even added a microwave and a tiny refrigerator, which Penelope had never dared open. The metal shelves were crammed full, leaving a narrow five-foot-long walkway in the middle of the room.

Now, that walkway was taken up by a body.

TWO

Penelope stared at the prone body of a young man in a paint-stained white linen shirt, black jeans, and white sneakers. His pale skin had a gray tinge, and it was that color that jolted her back into action.

"Call 9-1-1," she said, brushing past Esther's chair and using the metal shelves for balance so she could reach the man's head without stepping on his back. He wasn't moving. Behind her, she could hear Esther giving the dispatcher their location. Crouching down, she reached under and pressed on the man's warm neck. Blood rushed in her own ears, but she couldn't feel any movement under Jean-Philippe's warm skin. "I don't feel a pulse and he's not breathing."

Esther relayed that to the dispatcher, then said, "She wants you to start CPR."

There wasn't enough room for Penelope to flip him over in the closet, so she scrambled to the door, grabbed the cuffs of Jean-Philippe's jeans, and dragged him out into the room. As she rolled his limp body, she finally remembered the training from the class she'd taken. "Find a librarian, tell them what's happened, and have everyone with CPR training get in here." The paramedics would take at least ten minutes to arrive. Performing manual chest compressions wore people out quickly. Even firefighters switched to a new person every few minutes, and they were paid to stay in peak condition.

Interlacing her fingers over Jean-Philippe's sternum, Penelope locked her elbows and bent at the waist, chanting along with the song to set a good rhythm.

Stayin' Alive gave the perfect CPR beat, but Penelope was pretty sure Jean-Philippe was already dead.

BY THE TIME the paramedics arrived, Penelope's back ached and Jean-Philippe still didn't have a pulse. Four other adults in the library had assisted, which meant she'd been doing chest compressions for less than five minutes total, but she was exhausted. After the paramedics rushed out of the room, she sat down in the corner next to Esther, hugging Brutus.

The other members of the life drawing class clustered by the door, speaking in hushed voices to newcomers as they arrived. A tall, thin white woman close to Penelope's age with short black hair seemed especially stricken. She'd been one of the people doing chest compressions, so maybe it was just exhaustion that had her slumped in a chair. There was something about her that looked familiar, but Penelope couldn't put her finger on it. Or maybe it was the cosmetic surgery — the signs were subtle, but definitely present. Penelope had noticed that when people had the standard fillers and injections, the results made their faces somewhat similar, no matter the starting point.

It made everyone look vaguely like someone she'd met before.

When the woman looked up, she caught Penelope watching her. "I came by to take pictures for the traveling exhibit brochures..." she started to explain. Then she blinked. "I need to let my husband know." Without another word, she got to her feet, shouldered her purse, and made a path through the students clustered at the door.

"Where do I know her from?" Penelope didn't really care, but it was something to keep her from thinking about what had just happened.

Esther shook her head. "I've never seen her before."

They stared at the floor for another minute.

"I don't think..." Penelope let the sentence trail off. There was no reason to say it aloud. Esther had to be aware that Jean-Philippe had probably been dead before they found him.

"No. Probably not." Esther patted her shoulder. "But you did what you could."

Brutus leaned in and burped buttercream-frosting-scented breath into her face. Penelope glanced across the room and saw the empty plastic container and no sign of any food. "How many cupcakes did Brutus eat?"

"Two dozen. Paper wrappers and all." Esther was silent for a moment. "Well, minus one."

They stared at the plastic debris on the floor, left over from the automated external defibrillator pads. Penelope hadn't remembered the AED existed, much less that the library was likely to have one, but a librarian ran up from the first floor with the device. After they'd attached the pads, it had said "no shock advised" in a weird robotic voice. Penelope had taken that as a bad sign, but they'd kept doing chest compressions anyhow.

She tried to erase her visions of the unmoving body with memories of the artist as he'd been before. Full of drama, she thought, a figure larger than life. He'd once taken a bundle of junk mail with a shallow bow and a jaunty "Merci!" before returning to arguing with his assistant, a shy young woman in a ratty t-shirt who never made eye contact.

And now, there was nothing left beyond debris on the floor from their futile attempts to resuscitate him.

Penelope scratched Brutus's chest, sighed, and stood up. "I guess we should go." She felt oddly lightheaded, probably from the shock of it all. In a few minutes, she'd thrown away the trash on the floor and picked up Esther's cupcake holder. Brutus had thoughtfully removed all traces of frosting leftover when Esther had dropped them.

Wrinkling her nose at the smell of mice coming from the supply closet, Penelope pushed the door closed. "We should notify maintenance there's a rodent issue."

Esther nodded as they headed toward the elevator. "I'll call tomorrow. I'm surprised I didn't notice it when I dropped the cupcakes off earlier. But I was in a hurry then." She stabbed the elevator call button. "Let's go back to my place. You can call Jake to come over for moral support."

Penelope stopped on the verge of complaining she was a grown woman who didn't need to depend on any man. Because the truth was complicated, and she could be a strong woman while simultaneously wanting the shelter of her husband. She worked to make a joke about it. "How about immoral support instead?"

"That's a better idea. And where *is* your young man today?"

It felt good to think about *anything* other than what had just happened. "He's back at the storage facility, going through records of who bought things at the unclaimed unit auctions." Dealing with the slipshod record-keeping was part of Jake's missing painting case. When Joe Sayo auctioned off the contents, the winning bidder's information was written on a slip of paper that went into his jacket pocket. Then, as Joe's wife tidied the office, she transferred anything in his jacket to the receipts drawer.

Since the couple had been running the storage facility this way for fifty years, the "receipts drawer" and the paperwork associated with all the unit rentals now took up their own storage unit. Jake had been there every day that week. Penelope suspected everything would be perfectly ordered by the time he was done looking. "He thinks Yolanda and Eddie rented a storage unit when they moved out of their house."

Esther nodded. "That wouldn't surprise me. Yolanda had a hard time with that move. But that house had steps everywhere — even from the living room to the dining room — and Eddie couldn't manage stairs without help."

The elevator shuddered open. Esther rolled in. "I think we're due for a little extra something in our lemonade."

THREE

Twenty minutes later, they were seated on Esther's front porch, doctored lemonade on the table between them. Esther had a tray of tiny succulents to plant in miniature pots being given away to attendees at the charity auction over the weekend. While Esther handled the plants, Penelope filled the line of ceramic containers with potting soil.

Penelope paused in dirt shoveling to take a sip. She coughed, feeling the liquid burn a path to her stomach. "You know I still need to take care of a few pets after this, right?"

Another cupcake-scented burp came from Brutus, sprawled at her feet.

Esther waved her concern away. "You're not driving. By the time you walk there, you'll have burned it all off. And unless I miss my guess, that's your young man coming down the street now. He can finish up for you, if necessary."

Penelope twisted in her seat. Just the presence of Jake, with his general competence and well-worn laugh lines, loosened the tight band around her chest. She waved, then changed her mind and ran to meet him, Brutus galloping at her side.

Being hugged by Jake was like being protected from everything wrong with the world — at least until Brutus tried to join in and nearly sent them all into the street. With a laugh, Jake hugged the mastiff and gave him a quick pat on the shoulder. "Sorry, buddy, this isn't a great place to wrestle." He slipped one arm around Penelope's waist as they walked back to Esther. "You okay?"

"Yes." At Jake's raised eyebrow, she shrugged. "I'll be fine. I've just never had to use that CPR training before. Though I don't think it helped. Have you heard anything from the hospital?" Jake, as the former acting police chief, still knew all the first responders in town. He'd probably received multiple calls when people heard Penelope had been involved.

"He didn't make it. Sorry." They walked up the ramp to Esther's porch.

Penelope caught Esther's eye and shook her head.

Esther sighed as she poured another glass of lemonade for Jake. "I was pretty sure he was already dead when we got there, but you never know."

Jake sniffed his glass and blinked. "I guess this is appropriate for toasts."

Esther raised her tumbler. "To Jean-Philippe. He had questionable taste in food, and I doubt he grew up in Paris, but he was an outstanding artist and an excellent teacher. He will be missed."

All three sipped their drinks.

Penelope waited until they had put their glasses back down and Esther was showing Jake how to transplant the succulents. "I wonder what happened to him." Grabbing another handful of dirt, Penelope turned to Jake. "They'll do an autopsy, right?"

"It's an unattended death. Assuming his doctor hadn't

diagnosed him with some terminal illness, then yes, they'll perform an autopsy." He delicately maneuvered an echeveria into a pot. "There's a good chance we'll never know what happened."

"If there's any way to bend the data, they'll rule it natural causes," Esther predicted, adding another pot to the tray with more force than necessary. "The city's insurance will see to that."

Jake looked between the two women. "We shouldn't jump to conclusions just yet."

Penelope and Esther gave each other a significant look.

Sighing, Jake changed the subject. "Do I want to know why Brutus suddenly smells like cake?"

"Because while I was doing chest compressions, your dog ate nearly two dozen cupcakes." Penelope pushed the springy soil into the pot with her thumbs and frowned at Brutus. "Would have been nice if you'd left me one."

Brutus burped.

Handing the dirt-filled pot to Jake, Penelope winced. "We might need to let him out overnight. I'm sure it will all be fine in the end, but..."

"But that end may be in the wee hours of the morning," Jake finished for her. "No problem."

"Might as well take advantage of that mattress not letting you sleep."

Jake gave her a smile that bared his teeth. "The mattress is fine."

They frowned at each other theatrically for two seconds.

Penelope rolled her eyes and handed the next pot to Esther. "He'd rather have sleepless nights than deal with the mattress store." It was an old argument, but there was no heat to it. At some point, Jake would either go mattress shopping with her, or she would give up and buy one on her own. She just didn't want to make a unilateral decision. Not that her husband would complain if she bought a mattress he didn't like, but she wanted one he could get a good night's rest on.

Jake levered a tiny gasteria into the side of the nearly full pot. "I notice *you* don't have any trouble sleeping on it."

"That's because a clean conscience is the best pillow." Grabbing another handful of dirt, Penelope crammed it into a pot. "Whereas *you* need a better mattress." In truth, she kept so active during the day that she was asleep the moment her head hit the pillow.

"Children," Esther said, frowning at the two of them.

Penelope sat up and snapped her fingers. "*That's* where I'd seen her before!"

Jake raised an eyebrow and waited. Esther asked, "Who?"

"The woman with the pixie cut. The one who did CPR with us. She was on the phone in front of Jean-Philippe's house last week. That must have been her husband arguing with Jean-Philippe."

Esther nodded in understanding, because Penelope had told her about the scene. There was no point in having an artist-in-residence providing low-stakes drama if nobody heard about it, though Penelope and Esther did sometimes omit identifying details.

The argument in question had been well worth describing, mostly for the sartorial details. The woman's husband was a dapper man in a white shirt and green velvet vest and trousers, who looked anywhere between thirty and fifty years old at a distance, but whose hands revealed his age to be closer to sixty when he broke off arguing with the artist and strode over to snatch the mail Penelope had just delivered. Meanwhile, the woman with the pixie cut had ignored both men in favor of pacing next to a red convertible, cigarette in one hand and phone in the other as she demanded the person on the other end of the line "sit her down and staple her feet to the floor if necessary, or I swear I will fly out there and take these shots myself!" It was all larger than life, and Penelope was only sorry she couldn't stay to hear what the arguments were about.

Now, she sat back. "I'm glad I figured that out. Otherwise, it might have kept me up tonight." She cast a sly look at Jake. "Or maybe not. My clean conscience would have let me sleep anyhow."

Jake put the finished pot on the tray of party favors and turned to face Penelope. "*I'll* go mattress shopping if *you* promise to get your second shingles vaccine."

"I was going to do that anyway."

"Yes, but this way you'll do it sometime this century."

"Deal." Penelope had been avoiding the second vaccine because the first one had made her arm sore for a week — surely that was a sign that her immune system had reacted robustly and she didn't really need another shot. But if that's what it took to get Jake to the mattress store, she could handle a little pain. "I'll make an appointment tonight and we'll shop for a new mattress tomorrow."

"Good." Jake took another sip of lemonade and winced. "Hopefully, we'll be sober enough to drive by then."

FOUR

In the morning, Penelope shifted her schedule around so she had enough time for a quick trip to the mattress store. Now that she'd gotten Jake to agree, she didn't want to give him time to think up excuses not to go. But when she arrived home at ten o'clock as they'd arranged, he wasn't alone.

Detective Brianna Sanchez sat at the kitchen table, her long black hair swept up in a no-nonsense bun. Though Penelope liked Brianna, and Jake considered her a friend, they didn't have the sort of relationship in which she would drop by in the middle of the workday unless she needed something.

Penelope's heart rate increased. "Good morning, Brianna." The only reason Brianna would be here was if the police were asking questions about Jean-Philippe's death. Unless... Penelope narrowed her eyes at Jake.

He held up both hands, the picture of innocence. "She showed up on her own, I promise."

Brianna glanced between the two of them, but didn't say anything.

"I thought he might have tried to weasel out of going to buy a new mattress by calling you," Penelope explained. "The last time we were ready to go, Brian called with an emergency at work."

A hint of a smile appeared on the detective's face. "No more convenient calls from work now that he's retired?"

Jake pushed the plunger down on the French press and poured three mugs of coffee. "I have no idea what you're talking about."

"Uh huh." Penelope eyed him, but decided that conversation could wait until later. "Is this about what happened in the library yesterday?"

Brianna's professional look returned. "Yes." She got out her notebook and pen. "Do you mind telling me how you found him? I gather you aren't normally in the class."

So it *hadn't* been a natural death. Or at least, there were concerns. Penelope sat on her hands, wanting to ask questions, but knowing she had a better chance of getting information from Jake after Brianna left. "Esther asked me to bring Brutus. Their usual model couldn't make it, and she thought Brutus would be a good substitute."

If Penelope had been the detective, the interview would have been immediately sidetracked by questions about dogs and life drawing, but Brianna was more focussed. "Take me through what you did from the time you went into the room."

Picturing what had happened after Esther had found the body was easy, but rewinding a few minutes earlier took some effort. "I was letting Brutus sniff around while I looked at the artwork. We assumed Jean-Philippe had gone to the bathroom or something because his bag was there. Then Esther noticed the cupcakes were out."

Looking up from her notebook for the first time, Brianna said, "Cupcakes?"

Penelope explained about the cupcakes Esther had put in the supply closet earlier in the day. "They were supposed to be for after the class, but I guess Jean-Philippe's smoothie didn't fill him up." She couldn't read what Brianna was writing, which was really too bad. It would have helped Penelope know what had happened if she knew which gaps she was filling in.

"We didn't find any cupcakes in the room. Did Esther take them home?"

"No, Brutus did."

"Ah."

All three adults looked at the dog lying on his bed in the corner.

Brianna scribbled more notes. "No adverse effects?"

Penelope looked at Jake and waited. He shook his head. "Only what you'd expect after eating twenty-three cupcakes at once. The remains came out the other end at dawn... unless he's eaten other cupcake wrappers recently?" That last question was aimed at Penelope.

She shook her head. "Not that I know of." That was the best she could say. They tried to keep Brutus out of things, but he was big enough to push his way through most barriers and surprisingly fast for all his bulk. At least he was careful not to knock down children when he stole their treats.

Then the point of Brianna's question struck her. "You think Jean-Philippe was poisoned!"

Slowly, Brianna said, "The medical examiner smelled something in the stomach contents that he was concerned about. But we don't have the tests back yet, so please keep this to yourself." She looked at her notebook again. "You said something about smoothies?"

"Esther told me about them to explain why she thought Jean-Philippe wasn't from Paris."

Brianna paused mid-sip. After she finished drinking, she put her coffee down. "I don't think I understand."

Penelope explained Esther's theory that Jean-Philippe hadn't been from Paris based on his food choices. "I never really met him when he was alive, but I have to agree — he had that linen shirt that screamed 'Artist from Paris', but the shoes told a different story. Though I guess that's just relying on stereotypes. Still, every man I've ever met who wore linen shirts wore some sort of leather-soled shoe." She thought about it some more in the silence unbroken by Brianna. "Or sandals with socks. I don't know. Maybe young people in Paris wear sneakers these days. But have they stopped smoking?" She looked up to see Brianna staring at her and Jake smiling. "Sorry. I'm rambling."

The detective cleared her throat. "Did you recognize anyone on your way in?"

"The reference librarian, the one who's usually at that desk. She has a rat terrier named Pickles. She was talking to someone, but I didn't see their face." Penelope shrugged. "I would have seen more people, but Esther convinced me to go on the elevator with her because if it broke I'd get a chance to climb out through the hatch, but I'm not sure it even has a hatch. And it didn't break."

Jake's smile widened.

"I think that was the only person I saw, at least until we started CPR. Then there were a few people there, but I didn't really get any names. There was one woman who was there to take pictures. I think she knew him. But I don't know who she was."

Brianna nodded, clearly relieved to be back on solid ground. "And other than the cupcakes, did you see any food or drink?"

"No. I don't think there could have been anything out, or Jake's dog would have gotten into it."

Jake looked at the corner. "Our dog is a good dog."

Brutus, knowing his chances of treats went up when he heard that phrase, lifted his head hopefully. Penelope pulled a piece of freeze-dried liver from her pocket and tossed it across the room. The mastiff snatched it mid-air without getting up.

Brianna flipped her notebook closed and stood. "Thanks for the coffee. I'll get in touch if I have any other questions."

When Jake came back to the kitchen after showing Brianna to the door, Penelope looked at the time and then frowned at him. "Are you sure you didn't schedule that just to avoid going to the mattress store?"

"Just a happy coincidence. She called me to find out when you'd be home. I told her you'd be here soon, so she came by."

"Hmph." As an excuse, it was plausible. No doubt Brianna had Penelope's number saved somewhere, but Jake had been her boss and she'd always bounced ideas off him. Penelope checked the time. "Well, the good news is that we have *just* enough time to find out how hard you want your mattress to be."

"You don't want to postpone until we really have time to check them out?"

Penelope took his wrist and tugged. "And on the way, you can tell me what else Brianna said about Jean-Philippe."

FIVE

Penelope learned two things during their outing. The first was that the medical examiner was fairly certain Jean-Philippe had ingested poison hemlock. And the second was that she and Jake felt comfortable on entirely different mattresses.

"Try this one." Jake sprawled, eyes closed, on the plushest mattress in the store, his entire body sinking deep into the memory foam. "Does it make me less manly to want a soft mattress?"

Penelope sat and then flipped onto her knees as the bed tried to swallow her. "No, but it might make you a princess from a fairy tale."

Opening his eyes, Jake said, "I'm okay with that." He closed his eyes again. "How about I take a nap here and really try this out?"

"Let's check some others while we're here." Getting off the bed turned out to be a challenge, but she finally tumbled off the edge. The firm mattress in the next slot didn't threaten to eat her. When she leaned back, it felt like lying on the grass in the park. "Try this one. How do you get poison hemlock around here? That's the thing Sophocles drank, right?"

"Socrates."

Penelope shrugged. "Socrates, Sophocles..."

"Testi-cles," Jake offered, making it rhyme with the others.

Penelope nodded. "Some dead philosopher."

Jake made a noise that was halfway between a laugh and a cough. "Apparently, it grows wild all over the country." A few seconds later, the mattress shifted. "I'm not paying this much money for a plank covered by a quarter inch of padding. Tell me you don't find this comfortable."

"You have to admit this is more comfortable than the mattress we're currently sleeping on, and you didn't even want to come shopping with me." Penelope sat up and gave the bed a fond pat for not attempting to envelop her. "It can't be that common, or all those amateur foragers would be dropping dead constantly."

Jake pulled her to her feet, and they moved to the next aisle. "I think the taste and smell deter people." Squinting at the placard, he asked, "Do we care if the mattress is natural?"

"I say we find the most comfortable one we can afford." She looked longingly at the one Jake had just vetoed. "And we have about five minutes before that sales guy finishes up, so keep moving." She flopped down on another mattress. "What do you think about this one?"

Jake sat down, and the mattress bounced. "I think we might get seasick."

Penelope snorted. "Next."

When they reached the side of the room closest to the windows, Penelope glanced out to see a man getting into a small red convertible. "Hey, that's the guy!" She jackknifed off the mattress and landed on her feet.

Jake followed a little more slowly, but he joined her at the window. "What guy?"

"The one I saw arguing with Jean-Philippe in front of his house." She trotted toward the door as the car backed out of the space, ready to go introduce herself or at least get the license plate number.

Naturally, that was the moment the salesperson set his sights on her and Jake. He smiled broadly and held out his hand. "Hi there, folks! Sorry about the wait. My name is Walt. Can I answer any questions for you?"

"No, thanks. We'll be back later." Penelope dodged around him and ran onto the sidewalk just in time to see the car turn onto the road and speed up. "Bah." Even if she and Jake ran to their car, they'd never catch up in time.

Jake jogged up behind her as she came to a halt. "Esther's never going to believe me when I tell her you were the one who ran out of the store first."

"I thought I might be able to get the license plate, but the car went around the corner before I could get a good look."

Jake reached over her shoulder to show her his phone screen. "Then it's a good thing I got a picture through the window, isn't it?"

Penelope turned around and cupped his face. "You're the best princess ever." She grinned as his cheeks reddened. "And I promise I won't say that around other people."

"I'm man enough to take it." His fingers tapped on his phone, and then there was the whooshing sound of a text message being sent. "There. Brianna should be able to find out who he is." Jake put his phone in his pocket and took her arm. "Should we go back inside and let Walt tell us about the importance of organic cotton, or come back another day?"

"We'll have to come back later. I have to work." Penelope set her shoulders. "And I can't be late for my vaccine appointment this afternoon."

SIX

The nurse at the vaccine clinic finished the injection before Penelope realized what she was doing. "You're all set," she said, standing to open the door so Penelope could leave. The entire process had taken five minutes, and most of that had been spent reading the poster with symptoms of strokes.

After spending so much time and energy avoiding the thing, a pain-free, no-drama vaccine was a bit of a letdown. Penelope found herself hoping her arm would swell up overnight — just enough for Jake to notice, but not enough to actually cause problems with her job. In the meantime, she went to Esther's house. Brianna had asked her not to talk about the poisoning, but there was no reason she couldn't talk to Esther about *other* things. Besides, murder or no murder, the litter boxes needed to be scooped.

When Penelope arrived, Esther already had three visitors, all seated around the kitchen table with Pirate sprawled in the middle, watching them all with his one remaining eye. Everyone had paper and pen in front of them, as if they were in the middle of a meeting, though Penelope noticed they all had sketches of whatever portion of the cat faced them. Esther introduced her guests as she poured Penelope a glass of lemonade.

The young woman with the nose ring and black fingernail polish was Chiara. Penelope recognized her as a barista in the coffee shop downtown. From years of perusing baby name books while waiting in line at the supermarket checkout, Penelope knew the name Chiara meant bright or luminous, which seemed the opposite of the image Chiara projected. Penelope wondered if that was coincidence or rebellion. In any case, Chiara had drawn a series of clouds shaped like cat paws across the bottom of her paper.

Orla, a decade older, had the leggings, no-nonsense brown ponytail, and gigantic handbag that suggested she was taking a break between driving her children to activities. She'd caught Pirate's stubborn expression, which told Penelope someone had tried to move the cat off the table at some point.

Penelope recognized the third person, Roddy, because he often bagged her groceries. He was probably about Chiara's age, though she wouldn't have imagined they traveled in the same circles based on their clothing styles. Roddy looked ready to be promoted to the corporate office. Granted, he probably couldn't wear a nose ring or black fingernail polish at his job. Penelope tried to picture it, but her imagination failed. Roddy had drawn the silhouette of Pirate's head in the beam of a searchlight over a cluster of tall buildings. Penelope approved. She could come up with a backstory that included the reason Pirate only had three legs.

Knowing Roddy gave her the clue she needed to understand how they all fit together.

"You were all in Jean-Philippe's class?"

Esther nodded. "We were trying to remember anything

that might help the police find out who poisoned him." Her paper was titled *Suspects*, but was otherwise blank aside from the graceful arc of a cat's tail swooping across the bottom. "So we can save the police time."

So much for keeping the murder quiet. Just as well. Keeping that a secret would have made it impossible for Penelope to ask questions. "And?"

There was silence as the members of the art class looked at each other. Penelope took a piece of paper and a pen, drew a stick figure cat, then had to cross out one leg. That made it look like Pirate had a peg leg, so she added a boat with triangular sails underneath the cat. Then she got stuck drawing a flag with a skull and crossbones and ended up using a smiley face with two dog treats crossed under it. Penelope drew her head back and looked at the flag — maybe she'd use that design the next time she had her business cards redone.

Finally, Orla said, "I think it was Lilac."

Esther filled in the gaps. "Lilac Adams. She and Jean-Philippe had a falling out a couple weeks ago and he kicked her out of the class."

Penelope tried to imagine something related to life drawing that would cause an argument. Using the wrong charcoal? Shading things poorly? "What were they fighting about?"

Orla checked her watch before she answered. "Lilac kept trying to hire him for private lessons, and inviting him out to dinner. I heard her talking about a business plan. He was pretty good at ignoring her offers. But I think she had started bothering Maya. His assistant," she added, at Penelope's quizzical look.

"He was always protective of his assistant," Roddy

added. "When they went shopping together, he lifted the heavy items."

Esther gazed at the table. "I *think* Lilac and Jean-Philippe had been a couple at some point in the past. Though not recently."

Chiara snorted. "Friends with benefits, maybe, and then she caught feelings. JP wasn't the sort to do relationships. He probably thought he was safe with a teaching schedule that only kept him in one place for a few months at a time, and then Lilac followed him all over the country." She rubbed her fingers together in the common sign of cash. "Daddy has money."

"To be fair," Esther cut in, "Lilac's drawings are *very* good. She's done some exhibiting, and I don't think that's entirely because of her family's wealth."

Chiara nodded glumly, as if forced to concede this point against her will.

Penelope added an eye patch to the smiley face. "Was Jean-Philippe seeing someone else?" In her experience, spurned lovers held onto their belief all would be well right up to the point when the other person began dating someone else.

"Someone *new*?" Chiara clarified. "I don't think so. At least not someone important. But he definitely had an active..." She glanced up at Esther and rethought her word choices. "... dating life. He usually brought them to the coffee shop where I work the morning after."

"How many people are we talking about?"

Chiara looked at the ceiling as she counted on her fingers. Even Esther's eyebrows went up when Chiara ran out of fingers and switched hands. "Nine? Six women and three men. I never saw him with the same one twice."

Since Jean-Philippe had only been in town a little

under two months, that averaged to slightly more than one per week. Maybe it was because Penelope was older and had higher standards, but she hadn't even gone on a date in the six months before she met Jake. "That opens the suspect pool quite a bit."

"Does it? I think he learned his lesson with Lilac." Chiara looked up from the cat paw clouds that now had lines of rain. "Every time he came into the cafe with someone, he had the same routine. He would order the drinks, they would sit down, and then they would talk. Whatever he said, it worked every time. The other person would give him the 'Last night was great, but I think we should just be friends' speech — you get good at recognizing that one from a distance when you work in a coffee shop. We've all been trying to find out what he says, but it's always too busy to bus tables and eavesdrop when he comes in." She shook her head. "Not gonna lie — his shut-it-down game was strong. I think he had more trouble from the people he *didn't* sleep with. Other than Lilac, of course."

Penelope abandoned her Jolly Roger and made two columns on her paper, titled "Slept with" and "Not". She added Lilac Adams to the first column. "Who *didn't* he sleep with that was causing a problem?"

"Marianne, for one. I don't know her last name. She's in the beginning class. When she found out he came in for coffee every morning, she haunted the place. Then he started taking his coffee to go for a while and she eventually went away."

Penelope wrote "Marianne beginner class". Esther could provide her surname later. "Anyone else?"

"There were a couple other students in the beginner class who tried to get to know him better, but they gave up pretty quickly." Chiara added puddles on the ground from which cats were springing. The whole composition was cute and cuddly and exactly the opposite of how she dressed.

Orla nodded. While they'd been talking, she'd drawn tiny people running from the cat, as if Pirate was Godzilla taking a break in the middle of destroying a city. A minivan was crumpled beneath one delicate paw. Penelope noticed the minivan bore a strong resemblance to the one parked by the curb. "Jean-Philippe was pretty careful never to be alone with the younger students. I'm pretty sure that's why his assistant was always there with the beginners. She didn't do much assisting."

"More of a chaperone," Esther agreed.

"When did the beginners have their class?" Penelope added waves beneath her boat, and then a whale. Because she hadn't planned any of it, the whale ended up far smaller than the ship. Or even the flag.

"After ours." Roddy had begun adding details to his superhero city, the skyscrapers coming to life under his pen. He worked methodically from left to right, filling in all the white space. "There was a thirty-minute break in between. Chiara usually brought a carton of coffee from work and someone else would bake. While we were eating, Jean-Philippe pointed out what was working well in everyone's drawings." His pen stilled. "He really was a good teacher. I wish I'd told him that."

Esther reached over to pat his shoulder. "He saw how excited we all were that we were improving."

"I guess." Roddy began adding a balcony to the penthouse.

Orla looked at her watch again. "I have to go." She put her pen down and picked up her purse. "I don't think I have any information worth passing along, but if the police ask, you can give them my phone number."

That seemed to be the signal for the meeting to break up. While the others were slowly making their way to the door, Penelope went down the hall to scoop litter boxes. Pirate followed her so he could supervise, along with the rest of the cats.

Once she had finished, the cats all rushed to use the newly cleaned boxes, and Penelope was taking a break before starting on round two when Esther appeared in the doorway. "What do you think?" she asked as she rolled to a stop.

"I think finding nine different people to sleep with sounds exhausting," Penelope answered, "but it sounds like they ended things on good terms. What's Lilac Adams like?"

"Intense." Esther shifted in the chair to allow Frito to perch on her shoulder, the cat's pure white tail twitching. "Definitely fixated on Jean-Philippe, or... Fixated on having him as a sort of prize anyhow. I didn't get the feeling she actually knew him better than anyone else. Certainly not as well as his assistant, Maya, did. But I guess that's how obsession works."

Penelope tossed a ping-pong ball to the other side of the room, clearing out the box in front of her long enough to clean it. "From what your group said, I'm a little surprised it was Jean-Philippe who died and not Maya. It sounds like he used her as a shield."

"A bit," Esther said, though from her tone, she didn't really agree. Esther was a master of making everyone feel as if their opinions had been heard and validated and then steering consensus in the direction she'd been planning all along. "I don't think she was his shield as much as they were a team. Maya's an artist, too. Jean-Philippe had to step outside to take a call from his manager once, and Maya took over the class for twenty minutes. Did a good job, too. Similar advice in nearly identical words."

Penelope considered that as she swept the loose sand from the floor. "Like one of those old married couples, where they've done everything together so long they've merged into one." She and Jake would never hit that point. They both prized their independence too much.

Esther snorted. "They weren't quite that bad, but yes."

Another thought struck Penelope as one tabby chased the other out of the room. "Was it normal for Maya to miss your class? She wasn't there when the paramedics took Jean-Philippe away, was she?"

"She almost always made it there by the end of our class. Orla was right — Jean-Philippe was careful not to be alone with the younger students. But I don't think we can read anything into Maya not being there when we arrived. She seems like one of those people who gets involved in a task and forgets she's supposed to be somewhere else."

Penelope knew that sort of person well because she *was* that sort of person. She wondered how Maya functioned as an assistant with that sort of focus. Penelope had temped at enough businesses to know her own skills didn't lie in keeping another person on a timetable. Luckily, her son had never maintained the packed schedule so many other children seemed to have. He'd gotten together with his friends and played board games or built bike ramps on curbs. By the time he'd joined a few after-school activities in high school, he was old enough to arrange his own transportation and figure out where he needed to be.

She finally remembered the question she'd meant to ask earlier. "Remember when you said the room hadn't smelled like mice when you dropped off the cupcakes? I think that was the poison." That Jean-Philippe had been given poison hemlock wasn't public knowledge, so Penelope didn't explain about the research she'd done. "But who would eat or drink something that smelled like that?"

Esther frowned. "You think he drank it intentionally?" Then she shook her head. "No. There was no note and no theater. People don't drink poison and then just go about their day waiting to drop dead."

Penelope agreed with her. The suicide attempts she'd seen had come in two types. The first was of the "See what you made me do?" variety, often intended to cause as much guilt as possible to someone close. The other type tried to minimize the effects on the living as much as possible, wrapping up their affairs, leaving passwords and instructions on how to access bank accounts, and doing their best to keep their loved ones from discovering the body. Jean-Philippe didn't fit either case.

Which just left her with the obvious question. "Then why would he drink it?"

SEVEN

Penelope still hadn't answered that question by the time she left Esther's house to take Heidi for a run. The German shepherd was the perfect running partner — tireless, content to stay at Penelope's side, and willing to go anywhere Penelope wanted to take her. That last part was important, because it meant Penelope could head past the house where Jean-Philippe had lived without having to come up with an excuse.

When they reached Jean-Philippe's street, Penelope slowed to a walk. Heidi glanced up, her head cocked in mild confusion. "Let's walk for a while. Then we'll run back, I promise." Heidi did the dog equivalent of a shrug and paced by her side.

Because the neighborhood was older, the houses were more eclectic instead of the cookie cutter sameness of the newer housing tracts. Esther had been involved in finding a space for the artist in residence to live, and Penelope had taken pictures of the interiors of the houses that weren't wheelchair accessible, so Penelope knew more about this house, a slightly rundown Victorian, than she otherwise would. What had originally been the barn had been converted in the early twentieth century to a garage, and then fifty years later to a studio.

The house exterior had been painted entirely white — trim, walls, doors, and all. While that made the house look like the rental it was, Penelope understood. Painting the trim two or three complementary colors made the Victorian houses come to life, but it more than doubled the labor costs because everything needed to be masked or hand-brushed. Plus, before spending the effort carefully painting all the trim, much of it would need to be mended or replaced. Penelope loved the old Victorians dotted around town, but she was glad she didn't own one.

While the exterior was bland, the interior held the personality of the previous tenants. Every tiny room was painted a different bold color, with a mermaid mural in the kitchen and a green man mural in the largest bedroom, with phallic-looking trees that had left Penelope giggling for the rest of the afternoon. Penelope wasn't sure what a real artist would think of that mural, but there were two other bedrooms if the trees were too much to wake up to. Besides, anyone who taught art students had probably seen worse.

This afternoon, the crime scene technicians had parked their van in front of the house next to a police car, and a stream of people wandered in and out of the house carrying sealed plastic bags. From a distance, it looked like the bags held Bell jars of green liquid. Esther had said Jean-Philippe had been fond of smoothies — maybe that had been what contained the poison hemlock. If so, it must have been something he made at home, as the smoothies sold in the grocery store all came in plastic jugs.

Maybe it really had been an accident. If he'd inadvertently picked poison hemlock instead of wild parsley or carrots, he could have made the smoothie that killed him. Though that didn't explain how he didn't smell or taste the difference.

Loud music came from the back of the property where the studio was. When Penelope had heard the same music while delivering mail in the past few weeks, she'd assumed Jean-Philippe had chosen it. Had it been Maya all along? Or was Jean-Philippe's assistant playing his music while she mourned?

Unfortunately, jogging with a dog didn't give her a reason to go check out the studio. Still, it was good to know that the police seemed to think Jean-Philippe had been poisoned at home. She hadn't wanted to imagine the reference librarians capable of the deed, though they probably knew all about Socrates.

As Penelope and Heidi were one house away, a sleek motorcycle parked across the street, and a slim woman in black leathers removed her helmet, took a bouquet of roses from the hard case behind the seat, and walked toward the house. She tossed her head in such a way that her layered brown hair settled perfectly, like a model on a photoshoot. Motorcycles were common enough in town, especially during summer when the weather was nice, but solid cruisers suitable for long, comfortable rides were the norm, not racing machines that required the rider to lean forward. But it was the theatrics of her movements as much as the expensive, out-of-place motorcycle that clued Penelope in — this had to be Lilac Adams. She looked vaguely familiar, making Penelope wonder if she'd seen her somewhere before.

Lilac strode across the street with a gait that could

have come straight from a catwalk. At some point in her past, she'd studied to be a fashion model. Probably not professionally, though, Penelope thought. Not that she wasn't pretty, but much of her allure came from her makeup and the cut of her clothes. Plus, Lilac wasn't any taller than Penelope's five foot five, and the clothes designers wanted tall, emaciated women to show off creations that wouldn't look the same on anyone who didn't spend their life ensuring their body was all planes and hard angles.

A uniformed police officer Penelope didn't recognize moved to block Lilac's route to the door. "You're not allowed in there."

"But I have to..." Lilac held up the flowers to the unmoved officer.

"Sorry, ma'am." He pointed toward the driveway. "Add it to the others."

"But—" Lilac shrank back from his look and altered her course.

As she and Heidi moved past the fence of the neighboring yard, Penelope saw where the officer had pointed. A shrine of sorts had been set up, with cards, flowers, candles, sketches, and even a small clay woman that was still drying. Lilac knelt and began rearranging the display, moving all the other flowers to the sides in order to give her roses the prime location between two tall white candles, as if everything else was just a backdrop for her offering.

Having decided Penelope wasn't going to start running again anytime soon, Heidi took the opportunity to sniff at the flowers now sitting at the edge of the shrine, giving Penelope an excuse to stop walking. She spoke up. "Your art teacher was certainly well loved." In more ways than one, she thought, but she kept that to herself.

Lilac glanced up. "Jean-Philippe wasn't just a *teacher*. The world has lost a master, unparalleled in his field."

Not having enough training to distinguish between good and great, Penelope nodded, though she suspected Lilac might not find universal agreement with her thoughts. After all, if everyone considered him the best artist in the world, he probably wouldn't have been teaching a life drawing class in a small town. "We must have been fortunate to get him as our artist-in-residence. Were you in one of his classes?"

"He was going to be the cornerstone of the art community I'm building. In Napa." Lilac smoothed out the roses and stood. "I should have known someone would martyr him for his art."

Something in Lilac's movements reminded Penelope that she'd seen her before. "You were here yesterday morning," she blurted out before considering if that was a wise thing to do.

"No I wasn't." Her denial was instant, though she glanced back at the police officer standing in front of the house. "This is the first time I've been near this place in six weeks. And yesterday morning I was painting with watercolors in the park." She shrugged off her backpack and pulled out a notebook, flipping to one of the last pages. "See?"

Esther had mentioned Lilac's gift for drawing, and Lilac was equally proficient at watercolors. Penelope recognized the stand of trees in the park. The artist hadn't stuck to the scene in front of her, though, because a family of bears were climbing the trees and Penelope was fairly certain she would have heard if the town had been invaded by bears. "It's lovely," she said truthfully, as she handed the notebook back. "But it doesn't prove when you were there.

And I saw you coming through the gate yesterday morning."

"You couldn't have because I wasn't here." Lilac stared at her, as if she could change Penelope's memories through force of will.

Had Lilac sneaked into the house and poisoned Jean-Philippe? Penelope supposed that was possible, but it almost seemed as if Lilac was more worried about being seen near the house, not the poisoning. That thought sparked a question. "Did he have a restraining order against you or something like that?"

For a long moment, Penelope thought Lilac would continue the lie. Then the other woman blew out a breath and rolled her eyes. "Fine. Yes, I was here even though technically I have to stay at least fifty feet from the house." Lilac scowled at the house. "Maya — his assistant — convinced him to get a restraining order. Jean-Philippe didn't have a problem with me being there, but Maya has always hated me. Obviously, it doesn't matter *now*. And Jean-Philippe wasn't even here. He went to the late morning yoga class every day." She pushed a strand of hair away from her eyes with the back of one hand. "But if Maya finds out I was here yesterday, she'll probably have me arrested out of spite."

"But..." Another car drew up to the curb a little further down, and Penelope recognized Chief Purcell getting out. She leaned into the hedge she was standing next to, hoping he didn't look her way. At least she didn't have Brutus with her. She had no doubt Purcell would recognize the dog who had destroyed his expensive Italian shoes. Now would be a good time to wrap this up and leave. "But if you knew Jean-Philippe wasn't going to be here, why did you come by?"

Lilac's cheeks reddened. She mumbled a few syllables Penelope couldn't catch.

"What?"

"His future plans." This time she enunciated perfectly, though her face had flushed even more. "I wanted to find out where he was planning to go next, after this residency had ended. What position he was taking." Her model's posture returned. "For months, I've been working to get him to agree to join the colony as a founding member, and he kept putting me off. I needed to know what I was competing against. I *needed* him."

Penelope was torn between her desire to take this young woman by the shoulders and shake some sense into her, and her need to leave before Chief Purcell saw her. Surely Lilac could see that trailing around after a man — *any* man, but especially one who rejected her to the point of having a restraining order — was a waste of her time on earth. And yet... Penelope considered some of the self-sabotaging acts she'd done when she was younger, including leaving college before she had her degree. Some things everyone had to learn on their own.

"And? What position *had* he accepted?" Maybe a competitor for an artist-in-residence spot had taken matters into their own hands.

Confusion swept over Lilac's perfect features. "He *hadn't*. Not as far as I could tell." She frowned again. "He had brochures for trade schools." Those last two words were said with a mixture of disdain and disbelief. "People learning how to weld beams together don't care about *art*."

Penelope clamped her lips together until her need to refute Lilac's words had passed. They could discuss it later, if Lilac didn't pack her belongings and leave, now that Jean-Philippe was dead. "Could he have left the brochures around to..." *To throw you off the scent*, she'd been planning to say, but that seemed unnecessarily cruel. "To keep his real plans secret?"

Lilac shook her head, her hair swaying in a way that would have worked for a shampoo commercial. Penelope wondered briefly why her hair didn't show any signs of being squashed under a helmet and then chalked it up to physics behaving differently for the rich. "I doubt it. They were hidden under his mattress with his journal. If he was trying to misdirect me, he'd have left them in plain sight."

Over Lilac's shoulder, Penelope saw that Chief Purcell had stopped on his way into the house and was speaking to the uniformed officer who had turned Lilac away. If she was going to get away without him seeing her, Penelope needed to leave right now, but... "Do you have any idea why he would abandon his career?"

Before Lilac could reply, Chief Purcell's angry voice barked. "Ms. Standing? What are *you* doing here?"

Penelope pasted a smile on her face. "Just out for a jog. Have you met Heidi?" Right after she'd said it, she realized he almost certainly did know the shepherd, since Heidi had damaged a corpse and complicated a crime scene.

Purcell was not a dog lover. He gave Heidi only the briefest glance before focusing back on Penelope. "You have twenty seconds to get out of my sight before I arrest you."

Part of Penelope wanted to ask what the charges would be, but provoking a confrontation with the chief of police, who already disliked her, was counterproductive. Besides, Lilac had already pulled on her helmet and was almost back to her motorcycle; Penelope couldn't ask her more questions, anyway. "Have a good day! Come on, Heidi."

She turned and jogged away, Heidi trotting along at her side. "He's always grumpy," she explained to the dog as they ran. "It has nothing to do with you. You're a good girl."

Heidi flipped one ear to show she had heard this praise, though she didn't intend to let it go to her head,

Sinking into the soothing rhythm of her feet hitting the sidewalk, Penelope thought about what Lilac had said. "So why would an internationally famous artist plan to enroll in a trade school?"

EIGHT

Penelope's plans to talk to Esther about Jean-Philippe's possible career change were scuttled when she received a panicked call from a client whose hamster had gone missing. This wasn't too unusual — Hammy McGee was an escape artist, and Penelope had twice started a weekend of pet sitting to find a note explaining they weren't quite sure where Hammy was, though they were pretty sure he was in the house somewhere. But this time it was an emergency because Hammy's college-aged owner was driving the four hours home for the night so she could take Hammy back to live in the dorm.

"You've found him twice before," Janet said as she ushered Penelope in with relief. "We've looked everywhere and there's no sign of him."

Penelope's usual trick was to wait until midnight and then noisily eat a bag of chips while sitting on the floor in front of Hammy's cage. Hammy was a big fan of corn chips, which technically weren't supposed to be part of his diet. But who was going to deny him a treat when he sat up and begged? All those treats had made Hammy one of the best socialized hamsters Penelope had ever met. He'd only bitten her once, and that hadn't broken the skin. Unfortunately, Janet was hoping to have Hammy contained before Joline arrived home at eight o'clock.

So... hamsters were nocturnal, but there was a good chance all the activity of the search had woken Hammy early. And possibly made him a little grumpy — Penelope reminded herself to be careful if he appeared. "Do you have any corn chips?"

Janet threw her hands up. "You're a genius! I'll start laying a trail back to his cage."

Penelope caught up to her before she could spill any on the ground. The last thing they wanted was to give Hammy access to snacks where they couldn't grab him. "I'll take the bag in his room and see if that brings him out. While I do that, why don't you take another look behind the refrigerator and in the back of the cupboards with a flashlight?" Though the hamster normally went to ground in the room with his cage, Penelope wouldn't put it past him to make it downstairs where all the food was kept. Hammy could be sneaky.

Sitting on the floor, leaning against a bag of clean paper bedding, Penelope crinkled the top of the chip bag in one hand while she looked up Jean-Philippe's manager on her phone. It only took two links before she found the man who had been arguing with Jean-Philippe. Late middle-aged, with features that had a touch of uncanny valley confirming he'd had plastic surgery, Ricky Nash loved the limelight. The woman Penelope had done CPR with and also seen pacing by the convertible while smoking and yelling into her phone was in most of the posed pictures, looking slim and elegant, and Penelope learned Ricky's wife, Althea, was the publicist for the artists he managed. "Very convenient."

But Ricky was definitely the one who loved the limelight. There he was with movie stars at a charity gala, relaxed and smiling, as if all the cameras were there for him. At a gallery opening with Jean-Philippe, his blue velvet three-piece suit and crocodile boots were nearly staid compared to other outfits, though he fit in among the crowd in a way he wouldn't have had he been wearing a more conventional suit. At a documentary premiere, he was wearing a perfectly tailored tuxedo, the only hint of creativity coming from the subtle print of a starry sky on his bow tie. In one picture after another, he subtly stood out in every crowd, even though by rights he *should* have faded into the background.

"He's a chameleon, Hammy," Penelope murmured. She ate a corn chip. "Or the opposite, I guess. Chameleons disappear into their surroundings. He stands out." Finding more than photos took longer, but eventually she stumbled on an interview in a fine arts magazine.

Ricky Nash had graduated from a famous film school, intending to direct. But he'd found his real talents lay in guiding his friends' choices so they could get the funding for their next project. Five years before, he'd changed careers to manage artists instead of filmmakers. "Fewer egos involved," he'd suggested to the interviewer.

Jean-Philippe had been his first client, and his meteoric rise had propelled both of them to the top of their professions. Within a year, Nash had signed a full stable of artists, and he was able to pick and choose the ones he wanted to work with. From what Penelope could tell, he was very good at packaging the artist's persona, and that had more to do with the artist's career than their art. In reading about his list of clients, Penelope could pick out some similarities;

they were all good-looking, young, and hiding enough about themselves to add to the intrigue.

As an example, Jean-Philippe's origins were shrouded in mystery. Nash claimed to have discovered him working in a New York cafe with only three words of English, but nobody knew anything about his past before that. Another of Nash's artists, a woman who went by the moniker Arabelle, had supposedly been washed up on a beach in Oregon with no ability to speak and no memories of her past. Nash had heard about the haunting paintings she'd made in the hospital and had flown out to sign her on the spot.

Penelope put down her phone and dug out another chip from the bag, making as much noise as she could. "Nobody could be that gullible, could they?" Across the room, a paperback at the top of the stack slid to the side. "Even if you ignored the soap opera silliness of amnesia, how could a contract possibly be legal if one party doesn't know what name to sign? And if she was already such a great artist, she could have already been under contract with a different manager."

She crawled across the room and settled in front of the bookcase. "But it's a great story if you want to give someone an air of mystery without worrying they'll say something stupid to people at a party." Lifting the stack of paperbacks from the shelf, she found Hammy grooming his whiskers. "Hello there, little man. Your favorite person is coming to take you to her dorm today, so this game of hide-and-seek needs to stop now."

Hammy took two chips from her and shoved them into his cheek pouches. After that, he willingly climbed onto her hand. When she deposited him in his cage, he burrowed under a pile of paper bedding in the corner, presumably to continue his interrupted sleep. Penelope made sure all the clips on the cage were secure before she went downstairs to give Janet the bag of chips — somehow much less full now — and leave before Hammy escaped again.

Janet hugged her. "Thank you so much." She stepped back. "I have no idea how Joline is going to find him if he gets out in her dorm room. Don't be surprised if she wants to hire you to come up there and find him."

Penelope tapped the chip bag. "Just send her off with this. If that doesn't work, nothing will."

As she walked back home, Penelope thought about what she'd read. Ricky Nash deliberately cultivated an air of mystery about his clients. Probably it was all smoke and mirrors to attract publicity. But while the police were certainly looking into Jean-Philippe's current relationships to find a motive for murder, Penelope wondered what Jean-Philippe had been hiding in his past.

NINE

Jake met her at the door with a bottle of beer. He leaned in to hug her and whispered, "Brace yourself."

"Oh boy. This ought to be good," she murmured back. Then she took a quick sip of beer before following Jake into the kitchen, where Joann sat at the table, her hands neatly folded. Every strand of Joann's dark hair was gathered up in a neat bun, with not even a hint of gray. Her red sheath dress showed off her toned body and perfect posture. If it hadn't been for skin that had seen too much sun during her teens, she could easily have been mistaken for someone a decade younger.

But Penelope knew exactly how old Joann was, because Joann was a cousin of Penelope's ex-husband, and they had developed a frosty relationship on the first day they'd met. A mishap with a server had sent Penelope crashing into Joann, and the ensuing tumble had sent Penelope's then-fiance into gales of laughter. Since neither she nor Joann had been hurt, Penelope had been willing to admit the entire episode was funny, but Joann had never had a sense of humor when it came to herself.

Thirty years had gone by without a thaw. Things had worsened recently when Penelope's son had read erotic poetry at Joann's daughter's wedding. The bride and groom had put him up to it, and the rest of the wedding had been similarly hijacked at the direction of the couple, but in Joann's eyes, the fault lay with Penelope, who hadn't even been invited.

And now Joann was sitting in her kitchen.

Outside, Brutus leaned his nose against the glass slider confining him in the backyard. While it was fun to imagine letting the mastiff inside — Joann was *definitely* not a dog person — Penelope wanted to hear about whatever catastrophe was severe enough for Joann to put aside her enmity for the afternoon. "Joann! What an unexpected surprise!"

Had that been the hint of a smile, quickly hidden? If Joann had developed a sense of humor, Penelope was willing to cast aside thirty years of animosity and start fresh. But maybe it had just been a grimace.

"As I told your husband, I want to hire him to look into the authenticity of a painting."

Penelope looked over at Jake. While she was sure he could learn enough about *any* subject to take on such a case, art forgery was a little outside the usual realm clients brought to the fledgling detective agency. And he was already busy with three other cases.

But Jake hadn't sent Joann away, which gave Penelope a hint about the painting. "This is one of Jean-Philippe's?"

"Yes. Or it's supposed to be, anyway." Joann rearranged her hands on the table. "I commissioned a piece when Jean-Philippe arrived, a custom portrait of Emma and David. Henry and I are having a dinner party next week. I was planning to unveil the painting then, but I need to know if it's authentic first."

Understanding clicked. This was part of Joann's apology tour to her family, an effort to make up for the lies and manipulation she'd inflicted when she'd attempted to take over her daughter's wedding.

As an apology, a Jean-Philippe Blanchet original was a pretty good start. But only if it *was* a Jean-Philippe Blanchet original. And clearly, Joann had doubts.

"Why do you think it might be fake?"

"Because on the weekend he was supposedly in his studio working on the portrait, he was actually at a bed-and-breakfast with a 'friend.'" Her hands rose to sketch air quotes as she said that last word. "I know he hadn't done more than the rough sketch on Friday, because I saw the canvas. But when he gave the finished painting to me on Monday evening, the paint was just dry to the touch. Oil paints take at least eight hours to dry, even in perfect conditions."

Sometimes the most obvious answers were right. "Are you sure it's oil paint? Acrylics dry in minutes." Penelope knew that from helping her son paint the miniature pieces used in board games. After a while, Seth had insisted on doing them all himself — Penelope was quick, but too sloppy for her eleven-year-old son's standards.

"Positive. Oil paint smells entirely different."

Fair enough. Joann had been trained in drawing, and probably painting — she would know the difference. "What did Jean-Philippe say when you brought it up?" Anyone else might have been too embarrassed to ask, but not Joann.

"I never got a chance. It wasn't until over the weekend that I found out about the bed-and-breakfast, and I meant to ask yesterday, but by the time I got there..." She sighed. "I have a painting that may be the very last Jean-Philippe Blanchet ever made. Or it might be a forgery that he added his signature to. I have a certificate of authenticity, but I'm not sure that means anything."

The way she spoke, it sounded as if Joann was trying to decide whether to keep the painting in a vault or toss it in the trash. "Do you *like* it?"

Tiny frown lines showed up in the center of Joann's forehead and were quickly wiped away. "It looks like a real Blanchet, if that's what you're asking. Same color palette, same brush strokes, same details."

That *hadn't* been what Penelope had been asking, but she decided to go along with Joann's train of thought. "So you had no reason to believe he hadn't painted it until you found out he was away that weekend?"

"None at all."

Penelope glanced over at Jake and tried to read what he'd written on his notepad. The words were illegible at that distance, but now he was drawing a round bomb with "TNT" in block letters. That wasn't helpful at all. "So maybe he wasn't at the B&B the entire weekend. Or maybe he took his paints with him."

"We'll need to check on that," Jake added. "Do you know who he went there with?"

"Jacky Samba. She's in our drawing class."

Penelope wondered how Jean-Philippe decided between giving his lovers the brush off in the coffeeshop or taking them away for the weekend. Maybe the weekend getaway had *ended* with a trip to the coffeeshop. It all sounded far too complicated for her. One of the best parts of falling in love with Jake had been realizing that she wanted to spend the rest of her life with this one person.

That one person was even now getting up to show Joann out, so Penelope stood and said goodbye. While Jake walked Joann to the door, Penelope let Brutus inside. He gave her clothes an enthusiastic sniff, either because of the hamster or the corn chips or both. By the time Jake came back to the kitchen, Brutus had agreed to lie down on his bed in the corner in exchange for a liver treat.

Penelope kissed her husband's cheek on the way to opening the refrigerator. "Have I ever mentioned how much I love you?"

"Should I ask what brought that on, or just accept it?"

"Just thinking about how exhausting it would be to have a series of one-night stands." She took out the chicken breasts she'd left to marinate and put them on the counter. "Why were you rushing Joann out of here?"

"I already had the bed-and-breakfast details, and *you* were about to ruin a perfectly good detente by asking why it mattered if the painting was fake as long as she liked it." He turned the water on, filling the pot they used to cook pasta, the noise of the faucet forestalling her argument.

By the time six quarts of water had gone into the pot, Penelope had reluctantly agreed. "I would have just hung it on the wall and not worried about it. Who cares who painted it if you like it? But you're right, it's not worth arguing with Joann about it." She waited until he'd turned the burner on. "I'm surprised you didn't send her to someone else. Do you have the resources to handle a fourth case?"

He put an arm around her waist. "If I'd turned her away and rejected a perfectly good reason for you to ask a bunch of questions about Jean-Philippe Blanchet, you would have gone out and ordered the hardest mattress you could find. I'd never have a decent night's sleep ever again."

"You're a very wise man, Jake Wheeler."

As she stir-fried the chicken, Penelope told her husband what she'd learned from Lilac and her research on Ricky Nash while waiting for Hammy to come out of hiding. "If murder is usually committed by people close to the victim, Brianna will have at least a dozen suspects." She handed the wooden spoon to her husband. "Forgot to chop the veggies."

"From your barista's description of his morning routine, I'm not sure I'd call any of his one-night stands close to him. That's the whole point of a one-night stand. I'll allow the partner from the weekend getaway, though. And Lilac the stalker."

Penelope washed three carrots and began roll-cutting them after chopping off the ends and tossing them to Brutus. "Between Ricky Nash's roster of phonies and Joann's insistence that Jean-Philippe couldn't have painted the portrait she commissioned, it sounds like Jean-Philippe may have been a total fraud. Except Esther said he was really helping her with her drawing, and he couldn't have done that without being a real artist, right?"

"There's a long tradition of artists having students paint their works. Maybe it's something like that." Jake opened the cupboard next to the stove. "Any idea where the salt is?"

Penelope put the knife down and turned to look at the cupboard, noting the empty space where the salt should have been. "No idea. Maybe Brutus took it."

"Uh huh." Jake began searching through the other cupboards as Penelope went back to chopping carrots.

Usually, things ended up in the wrong place when she was thinking while her hands were busy putting things away. The last time she'd used the salt had been... Soup, from two nights ago. Remembering what she'd been thinking about was harder, because the list was nearly endless. They'd been talking about enrolling Brutus in the advanced tracking class. If Jake signed up for the local volunteer search and rescue team, he would need to be gone for a three-day class, which meant Penelope wouldn't have his help with the pet care business, so they'd been looking over the schedule to make sure that wouldn't be a problem.

They'd also talked about the soup itself, which had turned out really well that time. Since Penelope's approach to soup was to chop any vegetables that they needed to use up and add stock until it was about the right consistency, the results varied. That night, she'd wished she'd doubled the ingredients so she could have frozen some, especially since they had a surplus of plastic ice cream containers perfect for freezing individual servings. Ah. "Brutus might have left it in the freezer."

Jake shook his head and opened the freezer. "What do people without dogs do?"

Penelope gave an exaggerated shrug. "Buy less salt?" She went back to chopping carrots. "Don't artists who do that usually have their own school? Though there was that one guy who used to have shops in all the malls. I think he started with prints and then just dabbed a few splotches of paint here and there and signed it. Maybe Jean-Philippe did something like that."

Jake scraped the cooked chicken into a bowl. "Done with the carrots?"

"Right here." Penelope extended the cutting board to him, then began cutting celery.

"I think that guy outsourced the paint splotching, too. But I don't see how Jean-Philippe could have started with a print unless he had painted the thing first. So that's out." He stirred the carrots once, then turned to the refrigerator. "Forgot the ginger and garlic. Also, the onions."

Abandoning the celery, Penelope switched to chopping an onion into slivers. They had both minced ginger and minced garlic in tiny jars, a time-saver that horrified her son, who thought everyone should start with fresh cloves and ginger root. But they didn't use garlic or ginger fast enough, and Penelope got tired of throwing the desiccated pieces away. "Don't forget the salt."

"Very funny." The kitchen filled with the scent of ginger and garlic as Jake put the jars back into the refrigerator.

"I still think he could have painted it at the B&B. I mean, there's only so much time you can spend together as a couple before things get boring." The sound of carrots being stirred halted, making Penelope grin as she continued chopping. "Other people, I mean. Obviously, with *you*, I could spend the whole weekend in the bedroom and never even *think* about leaving."

"Nice save." The stirring began again. "The obvious answer is to ask Jacky Samba. If they spent the weekend together, she had to have noticed him painting a portrait. Do you know her?"

"Maybe?" She had a vague memory of a quiet woman hovering nervously behind her husband at a school board meeting, but that had been at least fifteen years earlier. "But Esther does." If Jean-Philippe hadn't been killed and Brutus had been allowed to be the life drawing model, Penelope would have met all the students in the class. "Why didn't Joann ask *her*? Or did she?"

Jake blew out a breath. "She did," he said, drawing out the word, "but I got the feeling the conversation devolved and Joann didn't trust that Jacky had told her the truth."

Penelope rolled her eyes, nearly slicing off the tip of her thumb. "That woman could irritate a saint."

Jake laughed. "Most of the town agrees with you."

"How did she end up with a child as sweet as Emma? It boggles the mind."

Jake cleared his throat. "For all you know, people might say that about you and Seth."

Penelope smiled at the cutting board. "Yes, but Seth *clearly* ended up with the best parts of me. Whereas I can't even find any good parts to Joann. It's a good thing Emma has Henry for her father. I'd hate to imagine how she would have turned out otherwise."

"Indeed." The garlic odor in the air took on an acrid tinge. "Are you about done fondling the onions over there?"

"Two seconds." As much as she wanted to put on a show of fast chopping, Penelope knew herself. All that would accomplish was her bleeding all over the food and having to re-bandage her finger ten times a day. "I'll get Esther to introduce me to Jacky tomorrow. How goes the great storage unit refiling?"

"Progress. I found the ledger for the right unit. After the Myersons moved to the assisted living facility, they stopped paying, probably because the bills were going to the old address. Though it wouldn't surprise me if they *had* tried to update their address and it never got changed. Remind me never to keep anything important at that place."

Penelope took the cutting board over and scraped the onions into the pan. Bits of blackened garlic waited among the carrots. "If we ever accumulate so much stuff that it won't fit in this house and garage, I'll drag the excess to the curb and tape a 'Free' sign on it myself."

"Noted. In any case, I found the date the unit would have gone for auction and the receipts from the next six auctions. Except..." Jake waited.

Penelope stopped chopping celery so she could look over her shoulder. "The contents were never sold? Is it all still *there*?"

"I had that thought, too, but no. Noodles?"

"In the fridge." An earlier invasion of pantry moths

meant nearly all the dry goods, including the soba noodles, were stored in the refrigerator after being opened.

As he rummaged through the bags taking up one of the vegetable drawers, Jake continued his explanation. "The unit was definitely cleared out at some point. When this all started, the Myersons were shown the current contents of the unit to prove their stuff was gone. But either the auction sale wasn't recorded at all, which..." He stood up, soba noodles in hand. "It's entirely possible. Their recordkeeping is a mess. Or someone came in and stole the entire contents. Which I suppose is possible, but I don't think most of the stuff was very valuable."

Penelope finished chopping celery and scraped it into the pan. "This was about five years ago, right? Before we met, anyhow."

"Somewhere around then."

"The Sayos used to have a lab named Theodore, a really nice dog. Always had a stuffed squirrel in his mouth, no matter where he went." She paused.

Jake added noodles to the boiling water. "I know you'll eventually say something relevant, so I'm just going to be over here, nodding supportively."

"You know it's no fun unless I can make you shake your head."

"You're the one who keeps telling me not to react when Brutus does something bad. I'll reward you when you get to the point."

Penelope laughed and gave up trying to bait him. "Okay. About five years ago, I was hired to take care of Theodore for a few days after Joe had a heart attack. He was in the ICU, Rita was there with him, and their daughter..." Penelope tried to remember the daughter's name, but it eluded her. She'd always been better at remembering the pets. "I can't remember her name. Really nice person, though. Anyhow, she was flying in from out of state and the flight was canceled and it was all a huge mess."

Jake set the timer for the noodles. "I'm with you so far."

"Right. So she shows up a couple days later than planned, finds out I've been taking care of Theodore longer than anticipated, and insists on paying me for the extra days." She shrugged. "I was just going to chalk it up to doing a good deed. Rita didn't need the extra stress, and it wasn't like I was going hungry."

"You didn't even have a place to live."

"I did more house-sitting then," she corrected. "Why pay rent when I could get other people to pay me to live in their house?" She shrugged again. "Anyhow. The daughter wrote me a check, except she actually had to write me *two* checks because on the first one, she wrote the wrong digits in the amount. She had pretty severe... whatever dyslexia with numbers is called."

"Dyscalculia."

"Yes, that. After she messed up the first one, she had me write the amount on the second one. It must be really hard going through life basically handing people blank checks and hoping they aren't going to rip you off."

"Agreed."

Penelope waited. After three seconds, she gave up. "Where's my treat?"

"What?"

"It's all in the timing. If you don't give the treat right away, there's no point. The link between the action you're trying to shape and the reward is broken."

Jake raised his eyebrows. "I was still waiting for you to get to the relevant part."

"It's obvious." Penelope thought back to what she'd said. Maybe she'd skipped a key step. "The Sayos' daughter..."

"Whose name you don't remember."

"Yes. She stayed and helped with the business for a few months while Joe was recovering. If *she* was helping with the auction..."

This time, Jake figured out where she was going right away. "If *she* was helping with the auction, she might have written the wrong unit number on the receipt." He stretched to reach into the bag of liver treats on top of the refrigerator and gave her one. "Well done."

Penelope laughed and tossed the chunk of freeze-dried liver to Brutus, who snatched it out of the air. "We need to have a talk about high-value treats."

Jake wrapped his arms around her from behind and nuzzled her neck, his voice dropping into a register that sent a shiver down her spine. "Oh, don't worry, there will be treats later. But..." He let go and crouched down to get the colander from the cabinet. "I don't want dinner to burn."

"I find your practical nature very sexy," Penelope admitted, admiring his form as he stood. "The Sayos' daughter could recognize the individual digits, but numbers seemed to be a concept that made no sense."

"So you think it's likely she transposed numbers instead of making them up entirely."

"Based on the first check she wrote me, yes." She looked at the vegetables in the pan and looked around for the sauce mixture that needed to go into the pan when the meat was added back. They'd both forgotten to mix it. Pulling a bowl from the cupboard, she said, "Look at us. If we're already forgetting most of the ingredients now, what are we going to be like when we get old? Can you reach the white wine vinegar?"

He handed her the bottle. "The good news is that we'll never be old. Every time we get close, the bar moves. And the better news is there's always takeout." He retrieved the soy sauce, sugar, and cornstarch. "After dinner, we can go over the receipts to see if any of them have the same numbers in a different order. And I'll see what I can find about this Ricky Nash character for you."

TEN

The next morning, Penelope jogged the four blocks between her most recent client and Esther's house, enjoying the way the sunlight filtered through the trees. Though she had a gap in her pet-sitting schedule that would have been the perfect amount of time to go back to the mattress shop, Jake was currently touring all the thrift stores within a hundred miles.

Armed with the knowledge that the unit number on the receipts might be transposed, he had contacted three buyers — luckily, the purchasers had written their own telephone numbers on the receipt, so at least those numbers were correct — and found the man who'd bought the contents of the Myersons' storage unit. The painting Jake had been hired to find hadn't been deemed valuable enough to waste time selling, so it had been donated to a thrift shop. But the buyer couldn't tell which shop, since he used a whole list of them. So now Jake was visiting every one on the list hoping the painting would still be there or the employees would remember who bought it.

As much as she wanted to sleep on a mattress without

springs poking her in the side, Penelope was glad to have the free time, because Esther had promised to introduce her to Jacky Samba. Penelope didn't even have to come up with an excuse to ask questions. With a client, even a client like Joann, she had an excuse to be nosy, which was good because subtlety had never been her strong point.

Esther was seated on her front porch with a woman in her forties dressed in a pantsuit with an array of shawls that looked both artsy and professional. Her purple hair was cropped short, and she unapologetically took up the space around her, in a way that many women never achieved. Definitely not the woman Penelope half-remembered from the school board meeting, unless she had redefined herself in the intervening years.

When Esther had taken care of the introductions, she poured Penelope a glass of lemonade and passed her a box holding small fabric tubes. "We're making cat toys to sell at the shelter fundraiser. Add a teaspoon of catnip to each one and I'll sew them closed."

Jacky lifted the permanent marker she was using to draw faces on the stack next to her. "Or you could do this if..." She trailed off as Esther shook her head.

Penelope smiled. "Esther doesn't appreciate my art."

Esther threaded ribbon around the opening of one tube, pulled it tight, and cut off the end. "We need recognizable features."

Jacky laughed and went back to drawing on fabric. "I suppose this is about Joann's portrait."

Hoping the hint of irritation in the other woman's voice was because of Joann, not herself, Penelope said, "She's concerned." There. That was a polite thing to say that didn't require her to pretend she and Joann got along.

Esther's lips twitched.

Jacky rolled her eyes. "Of course she is. If she were smart, she'd shut up about the whole thing. She has a certificate of authenticity, and it's not like anyone is going to claim it *isn't* a real Blanchet."

"Do you mind if I ask about that weekend?" On the way over, Penelope had reminded herself Jacky had been close to Jean-Philippe, if only for a weekend, and she might be grieving. She'd been prepared to tread carefully, but now she was starting to think that might not be necessary. Opening the plastic bag of catnip, Penelope inhaled deeply and sneezed. It was supposed to be in the mint family, but it just smelled dusty. She spooned some into a pouch and set it in front of Esther.

"Ask away." Jacky smiled ruefully. "Sorry, I'm supposed to be sobbing and threatening to throw myself off a bridge or something, right?" She sobered. "And I *am* sorry he's dead. He was a nice enough guy, and he didn't deserve to die. But we weren't a couple like *that*."

Since Jacky seemed to be the sort of person who prized bluntness, Penelope stopped trying to be delicate. "But you did go away with him for the weekend."

"I did, but not in the way you think." She sipped her drink and sat back in her chair. "I booked this romantic couple's getaway package at a bed-and-breakfast — horseback riding, chauffeured winery tours, hot tub, the whole nine yards. Non-refundable. And three days before we were supposed to go, my girlfriend dumped me for our best friend."

Penelope and Esther winced.

Jacky grimaced. "Clearly, I missed some signs along the way." She let out a long breath. "The fact that I'm more mad about her letting me pay non-refundable deposits when she *knew* we were breaking up than I am about her running off with someone else probably says it all." She paused to take another sip of lemonade. "But life goes on, so I went to drawing class like I always do. After class, JP was helping me fix the pose—the tilt of the hips was messing me up—and we got to talking and I told him about the weekend package I'd blown all this money on."

The spoon didn't fit into the next pouch, causing half the catnip to spill onto the table. Under Esther's gaze, Penelope used her finger to scoop it back onto the spoon and tried again.

"Anyhow, JP listened to me and said I should go anyway. And when I said it wouldn't be much fun with people giving me pitying looks all weekend, he offered to go along. Not as my partner, but just as a friend." She passed over a stack of pouches with cute faces drawn on them. "He said he was trying to avoid someone during the weekend, so I'd be doing him a favor. Maybe he just said that to make me feel better, but he did offer to pay half."

Penelope looked at the faces on the cat toys as she filled them. With just a few strokes of the pen, Jacky had given them personalities. Offering them to cats to drag around the house and hide under the sofa seemed a waste, especially since cats were just as happy with milk rings and crumpled balls of paper. But then again, maybe art was supposed to be ephemeral and common, not placed in stasis to be admired at set intervals. She would have to ask Jake's aunt for her opinion the next time they visited.

Jacky, not burdened with Penelope's musings about giving art to cats, continued. "And I thought, why not? I'd already made arrangements for my ex-husband to have the kids that weekend. So that's what we did. We had a blast. And we posted a ton of pictures on social media that made it look like we were there as a couple."

The satisfaction in Jacky's tone made Penelope wonder what *she* would have done if social media had been more common when she'd split with her ex-husband. Going away with her art teacher for the weekend might have seemed like a great idea. "So you spent the *entire* weekend together?"

"Almost every minute from Friday afternoon until we drove back on Monday morning. Amazing food, a tour of a vineyard on horseback, everything. It was actually the perfect thing to do right after a breakup. The staff was wonderful about it — I told them about the breakup when we checked in, and they went out of their way to make sure I had a good time. A bunch of wine, lots of fresh air, and I was too busy to mope." She laughed under her breath. "I may have convinced them to market it as a post-breakup package."

Esther nodded and clipped the end of the ribbon from another toy. "They could alternate weekends."

"Exactly!" Staring at the toy she'd just drawn on, Jacky frowned. "Hang on, I need to fix this. This marker's losing its point and it looks like this one has a black eye." She made a few deft pen strokes, then filled in an area. "There. That's better."

Penelope picked up the fabric. This toy had an eyepatch along with a mustache and goatee, somehow rendering it even cuter than the ones before it. Turning a mistake into a feature was a sign of a true master.

Jacky found another pen and continued on the next bit of fabric. "He definitely didn't have a canvas and paint in his duffel bag. And the only time we weren't together was the night he went off with the owner's friend." She sighed. "That was Sunday night. By then, I was delighted to have some time to myself. Spending that much time with another person isn't easy. And JP was..."

She stopped drawing and looked up. "I was going to say he was sort of shallow, but I don't think that was it. The *image* he maintained, that *French artist* shtick he was doing, was shallow. Whatever he was hiding under that might have been as deep as the ocean, but I never saw that part of him, even after spending the weekend together."

Remembering Esther's comments about Jean-Philippe not being who he seemed on the day they'd found him dead, Penelope looked over at Esther, who nodded and said, "I thought the same thing. He was hiding behind the stereotype, except for the times when he forgot or it was inconvenient. I don't think he was from Paris."

"I don't even think he was from France," Jacky said. "He cussed like someone from the east coast. New York, maybe."

Both Penelope and Esther stopped working and stared at her.

"On the vineyard tour, one of the regular horses was lame, so they put JP on the owner's mare. Everything was fine until near the end, when she got spooked by something and took off toward the barn, with JP hanging on for dear life." She snorted. "It's only funny because nobody got hurt, but you should have seen it — JP had a death grip on the horse's mane, and he was bouncing up and down as Portobello galloped over the hill and out of sight and all we could hear is JP yelling 'sh—'" She stopped. "Well, you can imagine."

Penelope could, indeed, imagine.

Jacky laughed again. "By the time the rest of us caught up with him, he was on foot, walking Portobello around to cool her off, and talking to her about the *carottes* he was feeding her. His French artist thing was back, and we all pretended we hadn't heard him swearing like a construction worker." She shrugged. "Now, I kind of wish I'd asked him about it, but at the time... I figured he probably had his reasons and if he wanted to pretend to be French, that was his business."

Torn between admiration for Jacky's live-and-let-live attitude and horror at her lack of curiosity, Penelope kept filling toys with catnip.

Esther shook her head. "I *knew* he wasn't from Paris."

Jacky nodded. "It was the white tennis shoes, wasn't it?"

"No, it was the smoothies. When has anyone who talked so much about Paris ignored good food?"

Jacky held up one finger. "That, I can explain. He couldn't taste or smell anything. A virus, a few years back. He said for a long time he found it really depressing to eat, to the point that his doctor almost hospitalized him. But he found he could drink shakes and smoothies and things like that, so he mixed up huge batches in advance and made sure to drink at least three every day."

That explained how he could have drunk poison hemlock without tasting it, Penelope realized. "Was that common knowledge? The lack of taste, not the smoothies."

"I don't think it was a secret." Jacky handed a corduroy mouse with a beret and a thin mustache to Penelope. Then she looked at Esther. "During one of the first classes, the entire room reeked of turpentine — I think somebody had spilled the jar in the supply closet — and he didn't even have the windows open when we came in. He said something then about not having a sense of smell, remember?"

Esther shook her head. "That must have been the day I was late." Looking at Penelope, she added, "One of the volunteers had left the book carts in the elevator so they would be in a convenient spot for setting up the Friends of the Library sale the next morning. It took me fifteen minutes to find someone to move them out of the way so I could get upstairs."

That would be the last time something like that happened, Penelope was sure. "That sort of information gets around." Actually, she was surprised Esther hadn't known, even though she hadn't been there. Esther heard about everything. But maybe all her sources hadn't talked about Jean-Philippe because she was in the class. "So really, anybody could have known how to poison him. Though they still would have needed to get access to the smoothie."

Esther added another finished toy to the growing pile next to her. With the red ribbon nearly the same color as blood, it looked like a mound of dead, misshapen creatures. The cats would love them. "Did you see the smoothie container there? Sometimes he brought it with him, but I don't think he did that day."

Penelope shook her head. "Though it could have been in his bag."

"I suppose." Esther sat up a little straighter. "I heard a rumor that he was killed with poison hemlock, and if the internet is to be believed, symptoms appear between twenty minutes and three hours after ingestion. Jean-Philippe..." She paused. "It feels a little silly to call him that now that I'm pretty sure he wasn't even French. Maya always called him JP, so I guess I'll use that. *JP* usually got to the library about thirty minutes before class started. If we got there fifteen minutes later..."

Leaning back while she thought about the timeline, Penelope said, "If someone poisoned his drink at the library, he had to have been there more than twenty minutes before we found him. A lot longer, because he wasn't just *starting* to show symptoms." Dumping a scoop of catnip into the next toy, she added, "Or the internet is lying to us."

"There should have been a period when he felt ill but wasn't yet incapacitated," Esther pointed out. "Why didn't he get help?"

Looking up with a frown, Penelope said slowly, "We already agreed he didn't die by suicide. Unless you've changed your mind?" There was some logic to the idea. Socrates had famously been murdered by poison hemlock, and from the accounts of his death, it hadn't been particularly painful.

"No way," Jacky cut in, putting down her pen. "I know people hide their pain and you never *really* know, but you can't convince me JP was suicidal."

"There could have been something else mixed in with the poison hemlock," Esther suggested. "So if he drank it at home, he would have come to the library, started setting up for class, and then collapsed."

"That seems to work out," Penelope agreed, "though it would help to know what else was in the smoothie. The reference librarians were down the hall, and he probably had a phone if he couldn't make it that far." And all this wasn't actually relevant to what she was supposed to be finding out — the authenticity of the painting. But she'd never been good at following directions. Something Jacky had said earlier came back to her. "Jacky, you said JP was trying to avoid someone that weekend. Did he say who?"

"No. I assumed it was Lilac. You've heard about her?"

"Yes." Lilac, with her model's composure and her obsession with JP — that might make sense, except for one thing. "But from everything I've heard, he didn't have a problem telling her to go away in person. It wasn't until she started bothering his assistant that they got a restraining order."

"It couldn't have been Lilac." Esther added another toy body to the pile. "Not unless she skipped the film festival she was so excited about. This was the weekend before last, correct?"

Jacky looked up from the steampunk goggles she was drawing on the next toy. "Yes."

Pointing to Penelope's phone, Esther said, "You should be able to look it up. There was a red carpet before the award ceremony. Lilac was a producer for one of the films, or something like that."

"That means she helped them get funding," Jacky explained without looking up. With the gears she had drawn, the toy now looked like a mechanical mouse.

Penelope put down the catnip and tapped at her phone. Lilac Freeburn had her own website — of course — with photos of her modeling haute couture, a tab to buy her artwork, and a whole section on upcoming appearances. The last section hadn't yet been updated, so Penelope was able to quickly find the name of the film festival and then search for photos of the event. It had lasted five days, and Lilac had been to both the opening ceremony on Wednesday and the awards banquet on Sunday evening. "By the time JP invited himself to the bed-and-breakfast, Lilac had to have been already out of town."

Jacky shrugged. "He never actually said it was Lilac he was hoping to avoid. I just assumed."

"Have either of you heard of anyone else he had problems with? Another ex-girlfriend, maybe?" She remembered what Chiara had said about his early morning cafe visits. "Or ex-boyfriends?"

Esther shook her head. "No."

Jacky added, "I don't even think he was worried about

Lilac. She was just sort of a nuisance he preferred to ignore."

Bundling the still unfilled toys into the box with the catnip, Penelope stood. "At least now I know for sure JP couldn't have painted that portrait for Joann. That gives me leverage." She thought about what Jake had said the evening before about the artist outsourcing all his work. "I need to go."

"You'll be careful, won't you? We don't know why he was killed." Esther pulled the ribbon tight and clipped off the ends.

"The police are welcome to figure out the murder," Penelope said. "I want to know what was going on with his paintings."

"Right," Esther said drily.

"Who are you going to talk to next?" Jacky asked.

"Someone who's been hiding her talents," Penelope replied.

ELEVEN

When Penelope arrived at the all-white Victorian, the police were gone, and there was no outward sign the house might have been a crime scene. A convertible with a rental sticker was parked behind the battered white van that had been there the day before. Though it might just as easily have been a friend or family member, Penelope's guess was Ricky Nash had arrived. She wanted to talk to him, but she needed to talk to Maya first.

A faint drumbeat came from behind the house, so Penelope skipped the front door and followed the stone pavers to the back of the lot. Weeds and overgrown bushes lining the path spoke of years of neglect, but just enough structure remained for Penelope to see that the large yard must have once been quite beautiful, with the herb spiral enjoying full sunlight near the house and a bench in the shade under a weeping willow. In the other corner, a depression in the earth next to a heap of rocks had probably been a pond. One hundred years ago, this would have been a lovely place to relax... for the people who employed others to maintain it all.

Though the broad windows of the studio were shut, with blobs of dusty paint suggesting they wouldn't budge in any weather, teen pop music escaped from the open hayloft door on the second story that had been leftover from the building's original use. "Oops, I did it again," a woman sang along, not entirely on key. Then her voice cut out for the next few lines, as if she were concentrating on something else, and picked up again in the next verse.

Penelope knocked on the sliding barn door. The volume of the music dropped, and a woman opened the door just enough to stand in the gap. Barefoot, in denim capris that showed pale white ankles, and a black t-shirt with bleach stains and smears of paint, Maya was in her early thirties. She was thin, but the type of thin that suggested skipped meals or ill health, not fitness. And, based on the clouds of alcohol that accompanied her and the way she leaned on the doorframe, she was also quite drunk. "Can I help you?"

"Maya? I'm Penelope Standing. I wondered if I could have a word with you." As the other woman pushed her wavy black hair back with one hand and left a streak of crimson behind, Penelope reconsidered. Getting sense out of drunk people was hit or miss. "Maybe we could set up a time to talk later?"

Maya pushed open the door and stepped back. "Better come in. Might not be a later. Sorry about the mess." The music switched to a boy band dance tune, and she scowled. "I *hate* this song. Hang on a sec."

As Maya walked across the room with exaggerated care to find different music, Penelope looked around the studio. The flooring of the loft had a large cutout, the open center making the studio feel bigger than it really was. A rickety wood ladder built by two-by-fours fastened to the wall provided access, though Penelope would have thought twice before trusting it with her weight. Three groups of canvases leaned against the wall near the front door, their surfaces turned away. Against the far wall next to a large sink was an old wooden dining table that might have been used in the house when it was new. Now it held an assortment of paints, brushes, mugs, speakers, a nearly empty bottle of bourbon, and cans of an off-brand soda called Hello Cola.

A stack of identical empty burger containers in the trash suggested that either there had been a late night run for food during a party or someone ate the same thing every day. Two easels were set up nearby, but only one held a canvas. Underneath the table was a mini refrigerator, and a corner of the room had been roughly framed to hold what Penelope assumed was a bathroom.

All in all, it had everything someone might need to spend their days painting.

After five attempts to find something she wanted to listen to, Maya gave up and turned off the music. "Can I get you something to drink...? Sorry, what did you say your name was again?"

"Penelope." The mugs on the table and piled in the sink seemed to have been used equally to rinse brushes and drink out of, so she thought better of her usual request for water. Esther would be happy she wasn't taking a drink from the person who could have most easily poisoned JP. "I'll have a soda, if you still have any."

On the way to the refrigerator, Maya flipped the sheet attached to the back of the easel over the canvas she'd been working on, though one corner of the fabric snagged at the top. "Can't have you looking at that, can I?" she muttered. "Ricky would have a cow." When she handed the can of soda to Penelope, she frowned. "You're not with the police, are you?"

"No."

"I didn't think so. You look too nice."

Penelope's spirits lifted. "Thank you."

"You're welcome." The words were said slowly, as if she had to concentrate. Maya sat heavily on a plastic patio chair. "Now, what do you want to talk about? Oh wait, let me get you a chair."

"That's fine. You stay there. I'll get it." As she walked past the easel, Penelope looked at the corner still exposed. In a grassy field, a flower with petals like a peacock's feathers leaned toward a yellow and white daisy, somehow managing to look both flirtatious and vain. Yet it was clearly a flower in the style of Jean-Philippe Blanchet.

And the paint still glistened wetly.

Penelope nodded to herself as she dusted off another patio chair and brought it over to sit near Maya. That answered one of her questions. "I wanted to talk to you about a painting done a couple of weeks ago. A portrait of a couple."

Maya sighed. "In oils, because that horrible woman insisted. Life's not fair. She gets the very last JP Blanchet ever painted, and JP insisted on giving her a *discount* because she was on the committee that chose him to come here." She slumped in the chair. "He thought this was the perfect place. And look what happened! JP's dead, and I'm about to get arrested."

Still thinking about the painting on the easel, Penelope asked, "Why would they arrest you? For fraud?"

"Ha!" Maya raised her mug in Penelope's direction. "They could have arrested JP for fraud. But I'm going to get arrested for murder. The police think I killed him." She drained the last of the mug and looked over at the bourbon. "I thought I should get drunk and paint today, since I won't be able to do either in the *slammer*." Her voice dropped an octave as she said the last word. Then a fluttering of wings in the loft distracted her. "Oh, look! He's back!"

Penelope got up and retrieved another soda from the refrigerator, handing it to Maya. If the other woman really was about to be arrested, she needed to sober up. "Here. Have some of this while you tell me why the police think you would want to kill JP."

"The neighbors heard us fighting that morning. Plus, I told them he left me everything in his will, which he said he had, but only because he wanted to make sure nothing went to his family. So the police think..." She trailed off as a white and black pigeon fluttered down from the hayloft to sit on the empty easel. "I'll miss you, Toes."

Penelope realized some of what she'd taken for splattered paint was actually bird droppings. This wasn't the first time a bird had perched on that spot. Though she wanted to find out more about the pigeon — Was it only one particular pigeon that came by? And why the name *Toes*? — Penelope recognized that her window for getting Maya to answer her questions was limited. Even if the police didn't show up, Maya looked ready to lie down and take a nap. "The neighbors heard you arguing and think what?"

"Oh, they think we broke up. Which I guess we sort of did. But not the way they assume." Maya opened the soda, took a long drink, and belched. "Excuse me."

"You weren't a couple," Penelope said, watching Maya's face for confirmation.

"Eww. No. Not like that." She took another gulp of soda. "He's not my type. Besides, JP was terrified of commitment and we've been working together for donkey's years." With a sniffle, she added softly, "I miss him. I didn't think I would, after he left."

"I'm sorry." With another person, Penelope would have offered a hug. But Maya seemed to have a bubble of space around her, and movements that screamed she didn't want to be touched. "You weren't a romantic couple, but you had a business arrangement, right?"

"I was his assistant." The words were said with no inflection, as if Maya had repeated them so many times a groove had worn into her brain.

Looking over at the pigeon perched on the other easel, Penelope snorted. "Did he paint *any* of them?"

Maya shook her head, but Penelope didn't think she was answering the question that had been asked. "No, no, no, no. You can't trick me like that. I'm not allowed to talk about that. Ricky would..." She shook her head again.

Which answered Penelope's question in a way. "Okay, how about *I* talk, and you tell me if I get something wrong." Maya had gone back to staring at the pigeon, who was shuffling back and forth on his perch, but at least she hadn't said no. "On the one hand, we have JP, who was better at convincing people he was an artist than he was at being one. It's a way to stand out in a crowd. People who buy art probably pay more if they can tell their friends stories about the artist."

"You have *no* idea," Maya muttered.

The pigeon hopped down to the ground and walked toward Maya.

"He had a flair for the dramatic, even pretending to be French because Americans have romantic ideas about French painters. But actually, he was from... New York?"

"Scranton, Pennsylvania," Maya corrected. She reached down and scooped up Toes, settling the bird on her lap.

Making a mental note to congratulate Jacky on her swearing geolocation prowess, Penelope stared at the pigeon. Now that the bird was closer, she could see he had extra feathers covering his feet. She hadn't seen a fancy pigeon flying free in years. "So JP was very good at acting like an artist, and I'm guessing he was fairly good at drawing people since he was more than competent as a teacher."

Maya looked up from scratching the pigeon's neck. "The most realistic drawings you've ever seen, when he could be bothered." She sighed. "But who wants hyperrealism? Even back before cameras, when they needed artists for portraits, you were supposed to make people better looking. And these days..."

These days, the phone in her pocket could do the same thing in the blink of an eye. "And on the other hand, there's you, an artist who..." Penelope waited to see how Maya would describe herself.

She didn't have to wait long. Maya had been dying to tell someone about this for a long time.

"Have you ever been to one of those exhibitions where they curate the guest list more closely than the art? Everybody's so busy trying to make sure everyone else knows what great taste they have, nobody ever really looks at what's in front of them. And if you think people value French painters higher than American painters, you should see the difference between men and everyone else." Maya picked up the pigeon from her lap and held it out to Penelope. "Can you hang on to him for a minute?"

"Sure." Penelope set Toes down in her lap, where he cooed and looked around from his new vantage.

"There's a contest." Maya climbed to her feet and crossed the room as she spoke, pulling two canvases from the group nearest the door. "Not all that prestigious, but the winner gets cash and there's free food the afternoon they do the judging." She held up the first painting in front of her as she came back.

"They judge the paintings while you're there?" Though the whimsical style Penelope associated with a Blanchet painting wasn't quite as pronounced, the image showed a girl diving from a cliff into the ocean below, wings unfurling and a pod of mermaids waiting in the water. "I'd always assumed they did that ahead of time."

"Most do, and those make a big deal about the judges not knowing any details of the artist until after the awards are given. But *this* one was all run by one local family, so they set their own rules. And even though they swore they didn't pay attention to the artist, *somehow*, every year, all the winners were men, from the cash prize down to the third runner-up. So I decided to make a point." She nodded at the visible painting. "Girl diving, acrylic on canvas. Entered in a contest under my name. Result: 'Technique sub-par, subject frivolous.'"

Dropping into her chair again, Maya swapped the other painting to the front. "Boy in flight, acrylic on canvas. Entered in the *same* contest as Jean-Philippe Blanchet, the most male and French name anyone could ever imagine. I hired the guy who worked in the coffee shop near my apartment to pretend to be him for the evening, and he went all out with a fake French accent. That was all it took." She snorted. "It was so over the top, I thought they'd never fall for it, but... Result: 'Outstanding, the vibrant color and impressive technique show the skills of a modern master.' It won the main prize."

Penelope traded Toes for the canvases. The arched-back pose of the girl and boy were the same, and the composition was very similar, though flipped. Where the girl was diving into an ocean, the boy dove from a towering rock into a meadow where trees held limbs to catch him. When put side by side, the colors were complementary, and they obviously belonged together as a set. Penelope set the canvases down next to the table. "I'd have waited until they awarded the prizes and then made a public announcement."

"That was the plan." Maya took a drink from her soda and burped again. Toes fluffed his feathers. "At least, that was the plan before I won enough money to pay both our rents."

"Ah." Penelope had been in dire financial straits often enough to understand the dilemma of proving she'd been right versus keeping the electricity on for another month.

"I'd thought I might win a ribbon. The main prize *always* went to a friend of the family, so I'd never even considered it." Maya frowned at her bare feet. "I think the whole contest was originally set up as a tax dodge. Anyhow, we figured we'd wait until the money was transferred and *then* tell everyone what had happened."

"Very practical."

Maya looked up and smiled. "You really are a very nice person."

"Thank you." Having occasionally paid the bills by catering events, Penelope had conversed with many inebriated strangers, and she was glad Maya was a pleasant drunk.

"But before that happened, a gallery owner approached JP about a showing." Maya shook her head. "So we agreed to hold off on the reveal just a little longer. And then..."

"And then somehow it was too late," Penelope suggested.

"And then Ricky showed up," Maya corrected with a

sigh. "He wanted to sign JP. Of course, JP couldn't actually sign a contract as Blanchet, so he said no. I don't know how Ricky figured it out — JP swore he didn't tell him — but a few days later, Ricky knocks on my door. He thinks the whole setup is brilliant *and* he can create a corporation so we don't have to keep dealing in cash or risk people asking about bank transfers to an account that had a different name. I figured, why not? I'd get to keep painting what I wanted, and JP could do whatever he wanted when he wasn't needed."

Maybe she'd become jaded as she got older, but Penelope saw some flaws in that plan. For one thing, Ricky Nash didn't seem like a beacon of altruism. "That kind of puts Ricky in the middle of everything, doesn't it?"

Maya glanced over at the bourbon, as if she wanted to go back to getting drunk, but she didn't get up. "Everyone always says you should get a lawyer before you sign a contract, but I didn't know any lawyers. I didn't even know what *kind* of lawyer I needed. And even if I had, I wouldn't have had any money to pay them."

Penelope could only nod. She had signed more than one contract without understanding all the terms.

"So JP and I signed on the dotted line. And suddenly Jean-Philippe Blanchet was famous, and JP and I were bound by non-disclosure agreements and I didn't own the name and I couldn't sell paintings 'with similar themes and composure' under a different name."

That last part was the big problem, Penelope knew. If Maya wanted to keep selling art, she would either have to keep producing paintings for Jean-Philippe Blanchet, or she would have to paint in a completely different style. Thinking back to what the neighbors had heard, as well as the brochures Lilac had found in JP's room, Penelope thought she knew part of what had happened. "JP wanted out?"

"It's been *five years.*" Maya slumped in her chair. "JP thought it was fun for the first couple of years, being famous and having everyone want to be with him. He had enough free time to do anything he wanted, as long as he was around for the events. We even traveled together, so it wouldn't be obvious the paintings were coming from someplace he wasn't staying."

"Thus the fiction of you being his assistant."

Maya gave a weak smile. "We tried just not saying anything at all, but I got tired of all the people letting me know my 'boyfriend' was cheating on me. It was easier if I said I worked for him. And it didn't look so weird if I asked questions about paintings being commissioned." She rolled her eyes. "Oil, not acrylic. He agreed to that one before I found out. I had to special order paints, and it's such a waste. I'll never use them before they go bad." She rubbed her face. "Though I guess I won't use *any* of the paints if I'm in prison."

At Maya's glum look, Penelope hurried to get the conversation back on track. "If JP had quit, where would that have left you?"

Maya's shoulders rose. "That's the thing. I don't know. *That* was why I called Ricky. I just wanted to know what would happen. I wasn't trying to stop JP from going." Her shoulders dropped. "I should have just hired a lawyer to look at the contract. Because the next thing I know, Ricky's telling JP he can't leave, and JP's yelling at me for telling Ricky."

"But..." Low voices came from the walkway in the yard. "Was JP just going to disappear? He would have had to tell Ricky eventually, wouldn't he?"

Maya rubbed her eyes on her sleeve. "JP kept saying it was all going to be fine, but I think he was going to leave and let me tell Ricky after he was gone. Now it's all a big mess. JP's dead. The cops think I killed him. And Ricky's going to sue me for everything I own if I tell anyone that Jean-Philippe Blanchet never existed." She stroked the pigeon in her lap.

"You need a lawyer," Penelope said, letting her voice take on what Seth called her "mom tone." "A criminal defense lawyer. Because there are times an NDA isn't enforceable, and this may be one of them."

A knock on the door echoed around the room. Maya kissed the pigeon's head and tossed him into the air. "Be safe, Toes." She watched him flap up to the hayloft. "I can't take that chance. My dad had a stroke last year and he'll get kicked out of the nursing facility if I don't pay. I'd rather go to prison than have that happen."

"But..." Penelope followed Maya to the door.

"It's okay," Maya assured her. She flung open the studio door to find three people on the other side.

Penelope knew Detectives Sanchez and Peterson. Then she recognized the third — even in casual clothes with two police detectives in front of him, Ricky Nash gave off the air of someone welcoming people to his exclusive nightclub. His too-perfect features had tipped Penelope off to a love of plastic surgery when she'd seen his picture, but up close, she couldn't see the usual signs at ears and brows. Perhaps a little puffiness from recent filler injections, but she wouldn't have noticed if she hadn't already known he was in his sixties.

She and Jake wouldn't look that young in another ten years, for which Penelope was grateful. As much as she tried to ignore the signs of aging, she'd earned every scar and wrinkle. Covering them up would have felt like she was denying the life she'd lived.

Brianna Sanchez raised one eyebrow when she saw Penelope behind Maya, but she kept to her script. "Miss Vane? We'd like you to come to the station with us."

Ricky spoke over the last word, his voice loud enough to be heard next door. "Maya, don't say a word. I'll have a lawyer meet you there, but keep your mouth shut until then."

From the way Brianna's jaw clenched, this wasn't the first time she'd dealt with Ricky Nash. But she ignored him and kept her voice pleasantly professional. "Do you have a pair of shoes you can put on?"

Ricky Nash repeated himself with the demeanor of a man not used to being ignored. "Not a word, Maya, do you hear me?"

While Maya sat on the ground and pulled on sandals, Penelope took the opportunity to lean toward Brianna. "You'll have to wait until she sobers up to talk to her."

The detective nodded in acknowledgement, but didn't turn her attention away from the artist. In just a few minutes, Maya was being walked to the car with Detective Peterson supporting her.

Though Penelope thought she might get away with staying behind and checking out the art studio, Ricky Nash held the door and waited. "What a disaster. This is the worst week of my life." Before Penelope could reply, he looked off into the distance. "Jonathan! It's Ricky Nash. I need you to drop everything and get out here."

He had Bluetooth earbuds in both ears, she realized. Giving up on her plan to snoop, she went into the yard and retraced her steps on the path, glancing back to see what the manager would do. Behind her, Ricky continued his conversation even as he rolled the door closed and used the key sitting in the latch to lock it. He pocketed the key. "I *know* you don't practice criminal law, but someone in that firm must..."

A not-unpleasant mixture of tobacco and orange blossom made Penelope turn to see Althea Nash, the woman who had helped try to save JP's life through CPR. She was seated on a garden bench, watching with something like satisfaction as Maya was led away. Noticing Penelope's look, she stood, every movement as graceful as a dancer's. "It's petty of me to enjoy this, I know, but some days petty is all you get."

Penelope had certainly had her share of days when that applied, though fewer once she'd started working for herself. But fairness required that she push back. "I don't think she had anything to do with JP's death."

"Oh, that." Althea waved that away with a flick of her wrist. "Of course not, but her transgressions aren't the sort of thing people go to jail for. Don't let her Little Miss Innocent act fool you." She glanced at Penelope's hands. "You're married? You'll want to keep her away from your husband."

Penelope tried to picture Jake and Maya together, but her imagination failed her. Even ignoring the marriage vows, which Jake took seriously, he was clear about his attraction to self-confident women near his own age. Maya had difficulty with eye contact. Jake would intimidate the heck out of Maya if he wasn't careful. "You're more his type," she admitted.

Althea smiled, her face lighting up. "Am I? That's the nicest thing anyone has said to me in weeks." Her attention was caught by movement on the building, and her smile turned into a cringe. "There are *birds* going into the studio."

When she turned her head, Penelope saw Toes perched

on the edge of the loft door. "That's just Toes. He doesn't count."

Althea looked away with a shudder. "Such filthy creatures. And the flapping..."

Having volunteered at the nearby raptor rehabilitation facility, Penelope respected their talons, and she had a crescent scar on her forearm from the bite of an overexcited parrot, but it was hard to imagine a *pigeon* harming anyone. Still, phobias were irrational by nature. "If you get the key from your husband, I can go inside and close the loft doors." That would give her a chance to poke around a bit more.

But Althea shook her head, keeping a wary eye on the pigeon, who still perched placidly above them. With a glance at the slim gold watch on her wrist, she said, "Excuse me. I have a call now that I can't miss." Without waiting for Penelope to respond, she punched a button on her phone and held it to her ear as she strode toward the front of the house. "Tom? It's Althea. Have you looked at the package I sent you this morning?"

Penelope followed more slowly in the hope that Ricky would finish his call and she'd be able to ask him a few questions. As she went by, she looked at the back of the house. Wide open French doors displayed a living room with a couch that had to be thirty years old. The rental came furnished. Penelope hoped the landlord wasn't charging extra for that.

With JP dead and Maya in police custody, the house shouldn't be left open. She started to detour, ready to close the French doors and maybe get a quick peek at the rest of the living room, but Ricky stalked past her into the house and began mixing a cocktail at the sideboard. "...then get him on a plane. I *know* this is a different state. There must be some way you can... Yes, that pro hac vice thing." He closed the doors, though his voice came through a gap in the frame. "So *find* a local lawyer to work with. I don't care. I just don't want everything to depend on some local hack who couldn't get a job anywhere else."

His dismissive attitude toward people who chose to live in a small town wasn't new. If he'd left the door open, she might have told him about the defense lawyer everyone called Hammerhead who had worked in a large firm and decided to move back to be near her parents. It had been years, and Vivica Hammer still received constant recruitment calls from her old firm and the attorneys she'd litigated against.

But given what she'd learned about Maya and the contract Ricky Nash had convinced her to sign, Penelope had to wonder if part of his concern was what might be made public by Maya's defense if he didn't control them.

If Maya told a local lawyer about the NDA, they might convince her it didn't apply. Then it would be more obvious she didn't have a motive to kill JP, at least not one based on jealousy or being fired from her job. Any two people who had to share a house might have reasons to kill each other, though that would probably be unplanned. Poisoning JP's drink spoke of premeditation.

Penelope gave up on her attempt to speak to Ricky. It appeared he was staying at the house, so she couldn't even waylay him on his way to his car.

As she walked around toward the front of the house where Althea paced back and forth on the sidewalk as she talked, Penelope cataloged all the ways someone could have gotten inside to spike JP's smoothie. Even without picking a lock — which would have been a piece of cake since these locks hadn't been changed in the last fifty years — Penelope could see at least five ways inside that wouldn't be noticeable afterward.

The kitchen window had a gap at the bottom where a screwdriver could be inserted to flip the latch. A second-floor balcony, with a handy trellis for climbing placed right next to it, had an open slider to the master bedroom. Another wisteria-covered trellis led to an open window on the second floor, and if that wasn't open, a few more feet up and another bit to the side was a propped open dormer window, which presumably allowed access to the attic. The wood around the side door going into the kitchen had been forced open at some point — the splintered wood was dusty and covered with cobwebs, so it hadn't been broken recently, but Penelope thought it wouldn't show signs if someone had pushed it open again. And finally, there was a basement entrance, which had been propped open with a bucket.

But none of that mattered, because Penelope was pretty sure there was at least one key under a flowerpot near the front door. In fact, it wouldn't have surprised her if there were five or six keys hidden in obvious places around the perimeter of the house. Hiding keys outside was a common practice in town, no matter how much Jake shook his head every time he saw it. And this had been a rental for so long, she suspected there were another few dozen keys out in the community.

Anyone could have gone inside and poisoned JP's smoothie. With Maya listening to music in the studio, it wouldn't have even required stealth, as long as JP wasn't around. And Lilac wouldn't be the only one who knew he regularly went to yoga in the morning.

If Penelope told Brianna the truth behind Jean-Philippe Blanchet, the detective would realize Maya didn't have much of a motive to kill JP, and the entire town had the means to do so. But Maya had said she'd rather go to prison than violate the non-disclosure agreement. Penelope could spill the beans *for* Maya, but then she'd be taking advantage of someone's inebriated state, even if it was for her own good.

Maybe Jake would know how to deal with this. Penelope had always been better at getting into legal hot water than getting out of it, which made them the perfect pair. In any case, she had to do *something*. Ricky Nash didn't have Maya's best interests at heart.

TWELVE

Jake arrived home just as Penelope was taking the casserole out of the oven. "Smells good in here!" He maneuvered a large rectangular frame wrapped in brown paper through the kitchen, pausing to kiss Penelope's cheek on the way. "I am covered in the grime of a thousand estate sales. Let me put this in the office and take a shower before I touch anything. Five minutes."

After Jake had dashed up the stairs, Penelope took Brutus with her into the office. If she stayed in the kitchen, waiting for Jake, she'd probably get distracted by something and leave Brutus unwatched in the vicinity of the casserole. This was safer for everyone.

Having thus justified her actions, she unwrapped the painting. "Oh."

The portrait Jake had been hired to find was of a green meadow with a small girl pointing at a dandelion. The meadow and the girl were still there, but now the sky was filled with spaceships and smoke, tentacled aliens crested the hill, and the flower had been replaced by a ray gun blasting a tentacle popping out of the ground.

Penelope took a step back to stand beside Brutus. "I don't know. I kind of like it like this." In Penelope's view, the original had been boring. If she wanted to see a child pointing at a dandelion, she would go to the park. This new version had a certain slapdash energy that appealed to her, though she suspected Esther would find fault with the artist's technique. But presumably, Jake's client had been hoping to find the artwork in its original condition.

She leaned closer. Was that a bandoliered Bigfoot in the distant tree line? And the girl's left hand had been painted silver as if she had a mechanical prosthesis.

Jake's voice coming from the kitchen interrupted her examination. "You okay with sandwiches for dinner?"

"I made — " Penelope looked to her left, only now realizing Brutus was gone. For such a large dog, he really was sneaky. "Sounds good." In some ways, it was a relief. She'd made the casserole to use up the eggplant she'd bought in a fit of optimism while grocery shopping, but she didn't really like eggplant unless it was smothered in tomato sauce and cheese, and they'd run out of mozzarella.

Closing the office door behind her to ensure Brutus didn't damage the painting, Penelope strolled back to the kitchen. "You found it!"

Jake looked up from the cutting board with a smile. His hair was still damp from the shower, and when she leaned in, she could smell the eucalyptus scent of his shampoo. "I'm not sure the Myersons are going to be happy about it, though."

Brutus lay on his bed in the corner, front paws crossed, with a studied look of innocence on his face.

"You haven't told them yet." Penelope grabbed a slice of Swiss cheese and then moved to the sink. The casserole dish had just a hint of baked sauce around the edge, but was otherwise completely clean. Brutus didn't give up on anything until he'd eaten as much as he could. She squirted dish soap into the pan, adding water so it could soak while they were eating dinner.

"I thought I'd look up some art restoration businesses and bring a list along with the painting in the morning. Damage control." He spread mustard on the bread, spicy for her, plain yellow for him. "What did you find out about Joann's painting? Real or fake?"

It occurred to Penelope that there was a way out of this ethical quandary of helping Maya without breaking her confidence. "The painting is exactly as authentic as every other Jean-Philippe Blanchet painting in existence."

Jake put down the knife and turned to face her. "That's oddly specific without actually answering the question."

"Mm." Penelope kept her mouth shut and waited.

He cocked his head and regarded her for a moment. "Okay, let me see if I can work it out." He layered sliced ham on the sandwiches. "Joann was fairly certain Jean-Philippe —"

"Let's call him JP for the sake of convenience," Penelope interjected.

Nodding, Jake started again. "Joann was fairly certain JP didn't have time to paint the portrait she received. But you say it's as authentic as the rest, which implies JP didn't paint *any* of them." He was silent for a moment as he worked. "His assistant? What's her name?"

"Maya."

"Right. I'm assuming Maya didn't go along on that B&B weekend." The top layer of bread went on both sandwiches, and then Jake busied himself cutting the crusts off his.

"Correct."

"So that makes her the obvious choice." With a flick of his wrist, he tossed the crusts over to Brutus, who caught them without getting up. "And from your uncharacteristic silence, I'm guessing there's an NDA involved. Though that wouldn't apply to you..."

Penelope accepted a plate from him and moved to the table. "She was a little drunk when we talked."

"Ah. You feel you may have taken advantage of her altered state." He slid into a chair across from her. "If the NDA was with JP, it may no longer apply. Depending on how the paintings were sold, I guess she *could* be charged with some sort of fraud, though even that would be a stretch since she wasn't the one doing the selling."

"JP's manager was Ricky Nash. He was there when Brianna took Maya away for questioning today." At his raised eyebrow, she expanded. "JP may have left everything to Maya in his will. Plus, the neighbors heard Maya and JP arguing. The police think he was firing her." She told him about the trade school brochure Lilac had seen.

The advantage of telling Jake specific information was that he knew how her mind worked and could fill in the gaps. "So JP wanted to stop pretending to be an artist. Which removes the obvious motive for Maya since he couldn't fire her if she was the one creating the paintings." He shook his head. "There's no way a non-disclosure agreement would be enforceable in this case, especially if one party is deceased."

"Maya's paying for her father's nursing care." That part wasn't covered under the confidentiality agreement. "She's not willing to jeopardize that." Penelope wrinkled her nose. "And Ricky Nash is hiring a lawyer for her. I think there may be a conflict of interest." She brightened. "But now that you've guessed everything without anybody telling you, maybe you could have a word with Detective Sanchez."

"After we eat."

Penelope nodded. "It gets stale faster when you cut the crusts off." She took a bite and frowned at the crumbs on her plate as she chewed. "The problem I'm having now is that nobody seems to have a motive to kill JP. Who wasn't even French, by the way."

"No?"

"He grew up in Pennsylvania. But Ricky and Maya had an incentive to keep him alive, at least until he stopped playing Jean-Philippe, and as far as I can tell, he was planning on finishing out his residency here first. Nobody he slept with seems to have parted on bad terms, other than maybe Lilac, and even she didn't want him dead."

Jake finished the rest of his sandwich. "Not even French. That's interesting."

"I really should have figured that out from his shoes, but I got distracted." Then Penelope eyed her husband. "Why do *you* think that's so interesting? I know why *I* think it's interesting, because who doesn't dream of convincing total strangers they're someone else? But that's not on your bucket list."

Jake's ever-growing list of things he wanted to do before he died included running a marathon, seeing the northern lights, and skydiving. Penelope preferred to run with dogs instead of people, agreed about the northern lights, and planned to someday learn fire spinning instead of jumping out of an airplane.

"You might find it fun for a day, but years? It's one thing to show up and play a role for a day or two, but JP gave up his entire life for this. Even if he was getting paid for it, that's a lot to ask. People who do things like that are usually running from something. Or running from some*one*."

A smile blossomed on Penelope's face. "So maybe nobody wanted to kill Jean-Philippe Blanchet, but someone could have had motive to harm JP, the former barista." She stood up and gathered their empty plates. "Have I ever told you how sexy you are when you solve puzzles?"

Jake raised one eyebrow. "If you want, I can bring the crossword upstairs with us tonight."

"Language of love, right there." Penelope fanned her face with one hand. "If I didn't have clients, I'd drag you to the bedroom right now. Oh, and you should probably call Detective Sanchez, so Maya doesn't spend the night in jail."

Jake took out his phone and dialed. While he was waiting for Brianna to answer, he leaned forward and whispered, "I'll even write the answers in *pen*."

Laughing, Penelope ran upstairs to brush her teeth. When she came back down, Jake was just concluding his call. "That was quick."

"There was a brawl at the Amber Tavern. They ran out of space in the holding cells, so they'd already sent Maya home to sober up. Brianna's going to talk to her tomorrow morning."

"You told her about Maya actually being Jean-Philippe? What did she say?"

The corner of his mouth twitched. "There may have been something about people interfering with her investigation. But she did sigh heavily in that way that means she's rethinking things." He shook his head. "She'll be busy half the night dealing with everyone involved in the punch-up."

Penelope dashed past him into the office to dig in the desk, where he kept a stack of business cards. "I'm going to drop by and give Maya one of Hammerhead's cards. She needs a lawyer who's looking out for *her* interests."

"While you're there, ask her what JP's real name is." Jake had followed her to the doorway of the office. When she looked up in surprise, he shrugged. "If we're going to meddle, we may as well meddle effectively."

Penelope kissed him on the cheek and went to do her evening visits.

THIRTEEN

The walk up the dark pathway to a tiny cottage would have been eerie if Penelope hadn't known the strangled gasps were caused by an elderly pug on the other side of the front door. Looky Lou shuffled forward when Penelope entered. "It's just me," she told the pug, standing still so he could sniff her shoes thoroughly.

Lou had started out with the typical bulging eyes of his breed, but time and a displeased cat had taken its toll; in the past twelve years, he'd lost one eye to a Siamese named Lovebug and the other to glaucoma. Now his name felt ironic, but Looky Lou didn't care. Eating, sleeping, and sniffing had been his three favorite things even when he'd had vision, and losing his eyes hadn't changed that. In fact, he seemed more lively now he'd had the second surgery.

"All done?"

Lou stood on her foot and kept sniffing.

"Sorry. No rush. I'll just stand here and think about why someone would want to kill an artist masquerading as another artist."

Lou snuffled his approval of this plan, inhaling deeply.

He gave her shoelace a tentative lick, suggesting that perhaps the artist had investigated a cat too closely.

After Lou had finished his perusal, Penelope took him outside for a potty break, fed him his hypoallergenic kibble, cleaned his ears, and gave him his anti-seizure medication. Lou had both a genial temperament and a long list of medical problems to balance it.

Carrying Lou over to his favorite bed, Penelope rubbed his graying face. "You're a good boy, Lou. Your mom will be home in a few hours. Behave yourself." His stertorous breathing had changed to snores before she'd made it out the door.

From Looky Lou's house, it was just a few blocks over to the all-white Victorian. When Penelope arrived, the ground floor of the house was awash with light. Though the red convertible was gone, she could see Ricky Nash gesturing with his hands in the living room, talking to someone. Althea must have taken the car somewhere. Penelope was halfway to the door when she realized Ricky was on the phone, at which point she diverted to go around the house. Sure enough, the studio glowed and Dolly Parton quietly begged Jolene not to steal her man. In Penelope's opinion, any man who could be lured away wasn't worth hanging onto, but she supposed Dolly's version made for a better song.

At Penelope's knock, the music stopped and then there was a clatter that sounded like a chair being knocked over. Penelope had almost decided to go inside to make sure Maya was okay when the door rolled opened, and Maya peeked out.

"Oh, it's you!" The young woman sounded relieved. She opened the door wider and waved Penelope in. "Come in before Ricky sees you!"

Penelope hastened inside, closing the door behind her, only then noticing the brush in Maya's hand. "Sorry, I didn't mean to disturb your painting..."

Maya tossed the brush onto the desk amid the other painting supplies. "I wasn't. But Ricky won't come out here and talk to me if he thinks I'm painting." She pulled a sheet off a television and game controller in front of a beanbag chair in the corner. "I'm taking a break from reality by harvesting fungus in Ant Farmageddon."

For once, Penelope felt knowledgeable about a video game. "I tried to keep aphids for a while, but they kept breaking out of my pasture. And then winter hit before I could get them back and everything died." She hadn't lasted long enough for the army ants to invade. At Maya's surprised look, she smiled. "My son worked on that game."

"Tell him he has a fan. I hang out with my friends every night. We have one of the longest running colonies in North America."

Penelope had never played the online version, but Seth assured her it was very popular. She was glad to hear Maya had some form of community — her life here seemed lonely, especially with JP gone. "I just wanted to give you this." She dug the lawyer's card out of her backpack. "I know Ricky was arranging for his lawyer to represent you, but I really think you should hire your own. She's very good."

Maya stared at the card for a moment before putting it in her pocket. "Thanks. My friends told me that, too." She shook her head at Penelope's unspoken question. "No, I haven't told them what I do, but they know the general outlines of what's going on."

As much as she wanted to force Maya to sit down and make the call right then, Penelope reined herself in. "While I'm here, do you happen to know what JP's real name was?"

After she said it, she realized it was an odd request and had to scramble to come up with a reason for her question. "Esther's putting together a memorial showing for his students here, and I wanted to invite his family, if that's possible."

As far as Penelope knew, Esther wasn't planning any such thing, but only because Penelope hadn't suggested it yet.

Maya squinted at the ceiling as she thought for a moment. "John Blanchard. Though I think he legally changed his name to John Phillips right before all this started." Maya waved her hand toward the easel. "He didn't want to keep his father's name. I got the feeling his dad wasn't in the picture much when JP was growing up. Changing his last name was a big deal because there was some old person with money in the family somewhere, but he said it was going to go to his father anyhow, so there was no point trying to suck up to anyone."

If JP had changed his name even before he took on the Jean-Philippe persona, Jake's theory about him running from something or someone could be right. "Did he ever seem worried about anyone finding him?"

"JP? He never worried about anything." A wave of sadness passed over Maya's features. "Who would ever want to hurt JP?"

Hopefully, they would figure that out before the killer hurt anyone else. Penelope put a comforting hand on Maya's shoulder. "Hire your own lawyer before Detective Sanchez brings you in again." She took a step back and waved. "I'll let you get back to playing."

After Maya had closed the door behind her, Penelope waited until she heard the latch click shut before leaving.

FOURTEEN

Back at home, seated sideways on the couch with her back pressed against Jake's shoulder and Brutus weighing down her feet, Penelope searched for information about JP under the names John Blanchard and John Phillips. Her initial query returned thousands of results, making her groan. "Why couldn't he have a less common name?"

"Like 'Penelope'?" Jake asked, not looking away from the curling match on television. Two players swept the ice madly as the stone headed toward its target.

"It would be a little odd for parents to name their son Penelope, but yes, that sort of thing. After you get past the famous and infamous people with that name, all of whom are too old to be JP, there's no way to distinguish the other 800 guys from each other. Why not name their child... I don't know, Hieronymus or Pieter with an i-e?"

"I'm glad that museum exhibit of Dutch painters wasn't a complete waste." They had made a pact a few months ago to do one educational thing every two weeks. Results had been mixed.

"So many men crowded into the paintings trying to

pretend they were busy doing something," Penelope sighed. "I temped in a couple offices like that, and I swear I was the only one doing any work."

"Could have been looking at harvesters instead."

Since Penelope had been the one pressing to go to the traveling exhibit of Dutch masters instead of Jake's suggestion of the tractor museum, she felt the need to defend her choice. "Someday we may need to retrieve a Dutch Renaissance painting, and when we find it in a thrift shop with aliens painted on it, we'll be about to talk about the themes and how the paints available at the time affected the mood, until the poor volunteer is so bored they give us the painting for free." She lifted her head from his shoulder so she could look at him. "Speaking of which, how much did you have to pay to get that one back?"

"Fifteen dollars. She offered to let me have the other one in the set for an extra five, but that one started out with a picture of a clown, so I declined."

"Good move." Penelope settled back against his shoulder.

There were gasps from the television as one team's stone knocked the other team's stone out of the circle. During the third replay from a different camera angle, Jake decreased the volume. "You know he grew up in Scranton, right? You might have better luck running a query on the name along with the high schools in the area."

"I knew there was a reason I kept you around." Penelope typed on the laptop as the announcers discussed stones, skips, and houses. "Ha! There we go." On her screen, four teenagers in stage makeup beamed as they looked out into the audience. "He played one of the leads in *Guys and Dolls*."

"If he sang like you, that *might* be a reason to leave town and change his name."

When Penelope tilted her head back, she caught Jake trying to hide a smile. "Keep that up and you and your crossword puzzles can sleep on the couch with Brutus." She burrowed deeper into the cushion. "Though it's more comfortable than the mattress, so you might be better off."

Jake wrapped his arm around her without turning away from the television. "But I could never sleep as well without you next to me."

"Nice save." Penelope closed the laptop. "Now that I have JP's full name and the high school he went to, I'll see if Esther can track down this rich relative he might have had." Esther belonged to multiple genealogy websites. Penelope slid her feet out from under the mastiff and set her laptop down. "How many more innings are left?"

"This is the last end." They watched as the final stone knocked the previous stone from the inner ring and slid to a halt.

"For a game that sounds so ridiculous, it really is mesmerizing. Everything is so smooth."

Jake thumbed the remote, causing the television to go dark. Then he reached into the couch cushions to pull out a large paperback of simple puzzles, the kind meant to keep children occupied. "I'm prepared." He waggled his eyebrows. "How's that for smooth?"

"When did you get that? No, scratch that, *where* did you get that?" Penelope laughed. "I haven't seen one of those in years."

"You married a man of mystery." He stood and extended a hand to help her to her feet. "I'll take care of the dog and meet you upstairs."

AT ESTHER'S house the next morning, Penelope sat on the floor, Frito draped over her shoulders, and played with Pirate while Esther worked on her laptop. The cat was missing a leg and an eye, but that didn't slow him down as he retrieved the ball Penelope threw across the room.

"Ah, there we go. John Blanchard, parents Steven Blanchard and Noemi Phillips-Blanchard. They divorced the year JP was born. Looks like Steven remarried soon after that, and JP had..." Esther paused to count. "Five half-siblings. Many pictures of Steven and his younger five children attending charity events, but no mention of his older son." She tapped some more. "It was his father's side of the family who had money?"

"That's what Maya said." Penelope pushed a tuft of white fur away from her eye, setting Frito off into fresh ecstasies of purring. "Does it have information about them?"

Esther snorted. "This website has information about everyone, whether they want it here or not." She clicked and typed as Pirate bounded off to fetch the ball again. "Oh, now this is interesting."

Penelope waited. Finally, she said, "You can't leave me hanging like that."

"Hm? Oh, sorry." Esther looked up from the screen. "I think you may be on to something here. Steven's father — JP's grandfather — is Gordon Blanchard, who attended the opening of a new hospital wing named after his late wife last summer. Steven and JP's five half-siblings are at his side in the picture."

"Big money." Penelope climbed to her feet, careful not to dislodge Frito.

"Old money," Esther corrected. "Railroads and oil. It

looks like Gordon has been doing his best to give it all away, but it's hard to tell how close he's come. Once you get to that level of wealth, it takes some spectacular effort to get rid of it all."

Sitting in the chair next to Esther, Penelope looked at the photo. All the smiling people standing next to the old man holding outsized scissors against a red ribbon had the professional polish that spoke of wealth. Judging a family based on one photo was an exercise in futility, but Penelope noted that none of the smiles reached their eyes. It could just have been that the sun was at a bad angle, but she was tempted to think there was something dark hiding in those expressions.

"But if JP changed his last name and was disinherited — whichever order that happened in — then money can't be a motive. Unless he'd made up with his father. Or his grandfather."

Esther switched to a different tab, this one showing an obituary. "If he and his father mended fences, it wasn't recently. Steven Blanchard died suddenly six months ago."

Scanning the two-page obituary, Penelope found the survived-by section. Five children were listed, but JP was conspicuously absent, both as John Blanchard and John Phillips. "It doesn't look like he did. Or else whoever was in charge of the obituary didn't admit it. That happens. My great-aunt died when she was eighty-five and her obituary only listed half her kids because they'd fallen out over Christmas cards the year before." It was a level of pettiness Penelope had to respect.

"Right, but look at this." Esther switched to another browser tab. "Four months ago, the school of medicine in Scranton announced the Noemi Phillips — that's JP's mother — memorial scholarship, given yearly to students intending to specialize in oncology. It was funded by Gordon Blanchard."

Penelope read over the announcement. "That sounds like... an apology, maybe?" It was hard to tell from the medical school's press release.

"It's a message of some kind, anyhow. At the very least, Gordon Blanchard was reaching out."

Penelope considered the information on the screen as she scratched Frito's chin. "So *maybe* there was a financial motive to bump off JP if it looked like he was going to be added to his grandfather's will. That's a lot of assumptions, though." She glanced at the wall clock. "I need to go. We're taking another trip to the mattress store."

Esther closed the laptop. "I have to get to yoga now, but I'll keep looking after I get back. If I find anything interesting, I'll text."

FIFTEEN

On their second mattress store visit, the single salesperson was once again busy with a customer. Penelope dragged Jake to the expensive corner. "Let's just try one of these mattresses that lets you dial in the firmness for each side. If we hate it, we don't have to justify the cost. If we love it, we can figure out if it's worth it to us."

Flopping down on the floor model, Penelope hit buttons on the remote and listened to the motor pump air in and out. It wasn't quite as comfortable as the more traditional firm mattresses, but it was far better than the marshmallow cloud Jake preferred.

Jake, meanwhile, was reading the brochure. "It comes with a fifteen-year warranty that's prorated after two years."

"Before you get into warranty specifics, see if you like it."

Jake sat down and examined the remote for the other side of the bed, methodically going through each of the settings. Then he lay back and adjusted it to his preferred level.

"What did you end up at?"

"Twenty. You?"

"Eighty-five." Penelope turned her head to look at him. "If I'd known we were this incompatible, I might not have gone out on that first date."

"And yet, here we are." He looked at the remote in his hand. "If we get a bed like this, you have to promise not to change my side in the middle of the night just because you're mad at me."

"Maybe that's why they advise couples never to go to bed angry. Although I think that saying predates this type of mattress. It's probably so you don't smother your spouse in their sleep."

"Probably." Jake dialed to a lower number. "It's still at least twice as much as I want to pay for a mattress."

Penelope rolled onto her side to face him. "How did it go with the Myersons? Were they happy to get their painting back, or mad about the extra bits?"

"Eddie can't see well enough to tell, Yolanda thought it was funny, and Irma was horrified. When I left, Yolanda and Irma were arguing about whether they should have it restored."

"Maybe Yolanda can get a print made of how it looks now, and Irma can get the original restored. Everyone can be happy."

"Very practical. I'll suggest it to them."

"Practical is my middle name."

"Yes." Jake stretched the word out until it no longer sounded like agreement. He tapped on his phone. "There's more than one complaint that this mattress squeaks."

"When it's adjusting? Who cares? You only have to set it once."

"No, squeaking during other activities."

Penelope cleared her throat. "That might be distracting. There's probably some way to fix that, though."

"Lubricant." Jake snorted, and then they were both laughing. "No, really. It says graphite solves the problem."

A chipper voice cut into their mirth. "How are you folks doing over here? Can I answer any questions for you?" It was the salesperson, a pale, clean-cut man in his thirties whose name badge reminded them his name was Walt.

Penelope tried to get her giggles under control while Jake sat up and cleared his throat. "If the batteries in the remote are dead, does the bed slowly deflate or maintain the last number entered?"

Walt brightened even further, as if he'd been waiting all day for a chance to talk technology with another man. "This is a smart bed. You don't even need the remote at all!" He whipped his phone from his pocket. "All you have to do is sign into the app, like so... Then you can adjust the bed. But that's just the start of it."

Jake leaned in, peering at the tiny screen.

"By using the sensors built into this model, the bed monitors how well you sleep. You can graph it over time, and then you can see here..."

Penelope rolled off the bed. She'd heard enough of Walt's spiel to veto the mattress. There was no way she was going to sleep on a mattress that was spying on her. Since Jake seemed entranced by the app, she left him there and wandered to the other side of the room, where there was a plain mattress that didn't care how she slept. It probably didn't squeak either.

Esther had sent a text. *Mighty Max is also Gordon Blanchard's son.*

Mighty Max was Max Ketley, a member of the Rose Garden Society. Penelope decided this was too important to leave to texting. With a glance at the other side of the store to make sure Jake and Walt were still occupied, she called

Esther. "How is that possible?" she asked in lieu of a greeting when Esther answered. "I never knew Max was adopted."

Max's father, Felix Ketley, had been the town's only dentist for many years. Felix had sponsored any community group that would put his name on the program or uniform, which was why the only two women's softball teams had been called the Clean Teeth and the Bright Smiles for many years. When Felix had finally retired, the teams had changed to Victorious Secrets and Blind Rage, and teammates shuffled according to which name they felt better suited them.

But for all Felix's professed civic mindedness, he had always made sure his name was somewhere in the credits. No anonymous donations for Felix Ketley. When Max, his son, had taken over the business, he'd continued the tradition, sponsoring community musicals, bowling leagues, and children's soccer — all with the Ketley name prominently displayed.

Esther's low hum told her there was more going on. "Remember the ads that came out last year ago for those DNA testing services? Alita bought one for everyone in the extended family."

"Yes. Oh." Penelope didn't bother asking how Esther knew that. Esther knew everything that went on in town. Penelope had viewed those home DNA kits as something interesting, but not for her. All the genealogy databases allowed the police to run comparisons — while Penelope doubted any of her crimes were worth collecting or analyzing trace DNA for, opting in seemed like a bad idea. Besides, she hadn't ruled out a future life of crime. It was never too late to change professions.

Max's wife had obviously not considered what might be revealed.

"Alita was planning on tracing the Ketleys back as far as she could, as a way to impress her father-in-law. Instead..."

"Nobody knew?"

"Presumably Deedee knew — or at least suspected — that Felix wasn't the father, but what could she do after everyone unwrapped their gifts?"

Imagining the panic Max's mother must have felt at seeing those DNA kits made Penelope cringe. "What a nightmare."

"Poor Alita. Apparently Felix is threatening to divorce his wife of fifty years, Deedee moved into Max and Alita's spare room, and Max isn't talking to his father. It's been nearly a year and things don't seem to be improving."

There was a moment of silence as they both considered how Alita's innocent gift had gone so wrong. Then Penelope remembered why Esther had told her about it in the first place. "Hang on. Max was on the selection committee for the artist in residence, wasn't he? What are the chances that the chosen artist just happened to be his secret biological nephew?" Jake could probably calculate the number, but Penelope was pretty sure it would be hard to write off as a coincidence.

"Low enough that I called Max's office to find out if he's in today. If we get there by three, we should be able to catch him. Can you make it?"

Looking at her schedule, Penelope said, "Yes, but I'll have to interrupt Jake's bonding session with Walt, so we have time to get everything done. Did you know they have apps for *mattresses* now?" She shook her head to clear it. "Never mind. I'll tell you about it later. See you at three."

SIXTEEN

When Penelope and Esther arrived at the dentist's office, asking to speak to Max about a personal matter, it had only taken the mention of JP's name to have Max usher them into a treatment room smelling strongly of antiseptic. He closed the door. Ultrasonic scalers and other dental instruments sat in their individual holders near the reclining chair in the middle of the room. Penelope wondered how hard it would be to learn how to use them, though she couldn't imagine sitting in one place and working on people's mouths all day.

"Of course I knew who he was!" Max whispered forcefully when Esther asked. "Why else would I have donated extra? The grant only covered one person, and he refused to come without his assistant. And I didn't even get any advertising space from it."

Esther sat up straighter in her wheelchair. "But that's entirely unethical. You had an undeclared bias. You should have recused yourself from the selection."

Max leaned against the wall. "Oh, please. Half the committee had some sort of bias. Frank wanted a fiber artist to boost sales at the fabric store. Leonore hoped we would choose the spray paint artist so she wouldn't have to worry about budgeting in graffiti cleanup at the high school this year. And Joann wanted someone she could use for bragging rights."

"Even so," Esther said, her voice heavy with disappointment.

Max shrank a bit. "It wasn't as if I set up the whole program to funnel money to him. I'd never even met him before. And he never knew who I was."

Penelope suddenly wondered if he'd had Esther as his teacher in kindergarten. It was entirely possible. She took pity on him and altered their line of questioning. "How did you know it was him? He was using a fake name."

"When the whole..." Max waved his hand. "...DNA test thing happened and my dad was being a complete jerk about it, Alita learned everything she could about my bio-dad. Partially, so we could find out if there was anything me and our kids should be monitoring for — hereditary cancers, that sort of thing — but we also just wanted to see what kind of people they were." He shook his head. "You would think we would have learned to leave well enough alone."

"Not good?" Would the ultrasonic scaler clean that grout in the corner of the shower where it was discolored? Penelope thought it might.

"It was..." For the first time, Max seemed at a loss for words. "I sent a letter to Gordon, my bio-dad, just to let him know... Know that I existed, I guess." Max shrugged. Then he rolled the equipment away from Penelope, but it was an automatic motion, as if he was used to keeping his work tools away from children who sat in the chair.

Esther's voice had lost its disappointed edge. "Deedee never told him?"

"From the little I could get my mother to tell me, it was just a one-time thing when she had gone to Orlando for a weekend with her friends. She met him in the hotel bar, things happened, and then she went home and never said a word to anyone. According to her, she and my dad had been struggling to have a baby — she thinks getting pregnant saved their marriage."

When she'd been younger and more certain of what was right, Penelope would have assumed Deedee was just trying to sway her son's opinion of her. But she'd seen the stress infertility placed on marriages when both partners wanted a child; having a secret affair was a terrible way to solve the problem, but Deedee could be right about it saving their marriage, at least until Alita had gifted everyone DNA kits.

Penelope couldn't have lived with that secret for decades, even to save an otherwise good marriage, but Deedee had been willing to make that trade and maybe that had been the right decision for her.

Except there were other people involved now. Penelope boosted herself into the reclining chair, noting indentations on the armrests where thousands of fingers had dug in. "How did Gordon react?"

"I got a letter from his lawyers telling me to cease attempting to contact him." Max shrugged again. "I didn't want his money and everything I read about Steven — my half-brother — and his kids made me want to steer clear of all of them. Steven put one woman in the hospital when he was driving drunk, and his kids were in the gossip columns for one thing after another. They weren't people I wanted my own kids around. The only one I was at all curious about was John, since he'd changed his name and disappeared. But I wrote the whole family off and decided not to worry about them. At least then."

"What changed?"

"Steven died, and I think something must have happened with his kids at the funeral. A couple months ago, I got another letter from his lawyers saying Gordon wanted to meet with me. Something about how he was re-evaluating his legacy. There was a strong undercurrent of 'you could end up inheriting money,' but it didn't come out and say it."

"You met with him?"

"No." Max let out a long breath. "I wasn't sure I should. My real father raised me, even if he has his head up his keister at the moment, so it wasn't as if I'd been missing out. And I didn't want Gordon to think I only wanted to meet him because of the money. Maybe that was stupid, but..." He shrugged. "There's no point in worrying about it now."

"Why?" Try as she might, Penelope couldn't see why JP's death should affect Max meeting his biological father.

Max looked between them in surprise. "Gordon's dead. I thought you knew."

Penelope and Esther looked at each other and shook their heads. "When did he die?" Penelope asked. "I didn't see anything about it online."

Esther narrowed her eyebrows and shook her head at Penelope's lack of tact. "May his memory be a blessing."

Max didn't seem offended. "Three, no, four days ago. Massive stroke caused by chronic hypertension. I got a call from the lawyer yesterday. Apparently, I'm going to be rich." He slumped on his stool.

For someone who had just inherited a pile of money from someone he'd never met, Max seemed nearly morose. Penelope paused to let Esther ask in a socially acceptable fashion, but her friend seemed lost for words. So she dove in. "You don't seem very excited about the money."

"I'm not. It's an absolute disaster."

"Because?"

"I've been saving and managing my investments so I could sell the practice and retire at the end of this year. I'm *tired* of being stuck in the office, looking at mouths all day long, having everyone look guilty every time they see me outside of work. My father was the one who wanted me to be a dentist in the first place. But if I retire *now*, he'll assume I'm rejecting him completely. I'll be stuck working here until he dies."

"Huh." Penelope considered that. Max was probably right about his father taking Max's retirement as a rejection. Without the inheritance, it would have just been a sign of success. With the inheritance, it might seem that Max was flaunting his new family connections.

"Besides," Max added, "have you ever seen those documentaries on people who win the lottery? Every one of them is miserable afterward."

Penelope agreed with his caution, though a part of her was glad she'd never been faced with the temptation. The other part of her pointed out she and Jake could get a custom non-spying mattress made for them if they had Gordon Blanchard levels of wealth. "You could always refuse it. Or give it away."

"I could, but what if Alita got sick and we needed money to fund her treatment? So it makes sense to keep at least some of it, but once you start down that path, it's impossible to say how much is really enough."

Assuming Max was being truthful about the inheritance, he didn't have a motive to kill JP. Still, it was good to be thorough. "So, how did you first get in touch with John Phillips?"

"The selection committee had the press packets for

everyone who applied. It wasn't a huge leap to go from John Phillips to Jean-Philippe, especially when I saw the photo. He had my son's eyes and jawline." His gaze flicked to Esther. "So I chose his application because I was curious. At least we didn't end up with the woman who wanted to shave dogs and use their fur to knit sweaters for all the trees downtown."

Esther sighed. "I suppose that is a bonus."

Max glanced at his watch. "Are we done? I'm the umpire for the Teenie Tots T-ball game and I have to pick my granddaughter up from school first."

Jolted from her reverie about whether it would be possible to use mastiff hair in knitting, Penelope pulled her thoughts back to the conversation.

"Did you and JP ever talk? While he was here, I mean."

"We met at the welcome dinner, though it wasn't like I could have said anything even if I wanted to. He was pretending to be French. But..." Frowning, Max continued. "He winked at me. I don't know. Maybe he was just doing that French flirting thing, but I think he may have known who I was."

"And you never talked after that?"

"No. I still hadn't made up my mind about whether I wanted to know more about anyone in the family." He waved his hand in the general direction of the library. "And then it was too late."

SEVENTEEN

Penelope jogged along the park path with Heidi by her side. The German shepherd's ears flopped with every step, but they never stopped swiveling, warning Penelope of every squirrel, bird, and person that might be a threat. Heidi took her protection duties seriously.

But when Heidi's gaze locked onto something on the other side of the park and she gained a spring in her step, Penelope wasn't surprised to see Jake jogging to intercept them. Most dogs liked Jake, but Heidi adored him, partially because Jake would sprint with her when they ran together. Penelope could keep a reasonable pace for multiple miles, but her legs weren't long enough to put on serious speed.

"Come here often?" Jake asked, slowing to her pace as he caught up.

"It's sort of comforting, knowing how terrible you are at flirting with strange women."

"And yet, I managed to get the strangest woman around to marry me. So I must not be *that* bad at it." He reached over to take Heidi's leash. "Let me take her on a quick lap and then you can tell me all about Mighty Max."

As Jake and Heidi bounded forward, Penelope dropped to a walk on the shaded path to watch them. Someday, Jake wouldn't be able to sprint around the park, looking like he was still in his prime, but for now, his movements were beautiful. Heidi dashed next to him, so excited that she nearly pulled at the leash. Both of them were panting when they finished the lap and pulled up next to her.

Jake flopped down on his back in the grass. "I think I'm faster now than I was in high school."

"Just don't hurt yourself trying to prove it. You definitely don't heal like an eighteen-year-old." Penelope grasped his hand to help him to his feet, resisting his attempt to pull her down with him. "If you stay there, your muscles are going to stiffen, and I haven't quite reached the stage of thinking the smell of Bengay is sexy."

"You should work on that. Think of all the money we could save on massage oils."

Penelope grinned and told him what she'd learned about Max and Gordon's change of heart after Steven's death.

Jake listened in silence until she finished. "So, if Gordon intended to split his estate equally among his heirs, the other heirs *might* have had a motive to get rid of JP."

"Yes."

"But we don't have any evidence that any of them have ever been in town. Aside from JP and Mighty Max."

"Right. I can't imagine they would blend in much better than Lilac, but someone would have to check their alibis and all the flight information. It sounds like a lot of tedious work that someone with a badge and a warrant will have to do." This was not the first time Penelope had realized she was temperamentally unsuited for certain jobs.

"You realize this may mean Maya inherits a *lot* of

money. It will depend on how Gordon's will is written — sometimes there's a clause specifying the beneficiary needs to survive some number of hours or days past the death of the testator, so they aren't trying to figure out who died first in an accident. But she could have millions of motives."

"Chief Purcell will *love* that."

Jake nodded without commenting. "And Max?"

They stopped to let Heidi take a potty break. Penelope looked at her husband as she tore a bag off the roll attached to the leash. "Max doesn't have a motive. He's never even met Gordon. And he doesn't want the money."

"You only have Max's word for that," Jake pointed out. "It's a little suspicious that he didn't say anything about being related to JP until Esther found out. He's had time to come up with a good story."

Crouching to clean up after Heidi, Penelope considered that. "But..."

"You only have Max's word that JP and Maya applied for the artist-in-residence program on their own. It's entirely possible that Max contacted JP and lured him here, intending to kill him."

"Max? I can't believe Max would do something like that." Penelope stood, tied off the bag, and tossed it into the trash receptacle. "Though he *is* a dentist." She saw Jake try to hide his grin at her slander of an entire profession. "No. I just can't see it. How about you? Did you learn anything useful about your cases today?"

They had reached the edge of the park, and Jake turned with her toward Heidi's home. "I spent three hours looking through boxes in Ella's attic."

"I'm surprised she was willing to pay you for those hours." Ella was the client with the missing doll, a creepy antique clown that Penelope would have never let into the house. But when Ella found out how much a similar doll had sold for at a recent auction, she'd hired Jake to find the collectable, which she thought had ended up with her estranged father when Ella's parents had split. Jake and Penelope wondered privately how much of her quest had to do with the doll, and how much had to do with embarrassing her father's second wife.

"I told her I wouldn't charge her unless I found it."

"How far did you get?"

"About a quarter of the way through. The doll was in a box labeled 'crap to donate,' so she's lucky it was still there." He paused to scrape some landscaping bark from the sidewalk. "It wasn't exactly in mint condition, but that's not my problem. We got paid enough to afford the fancy supermarket wine with dinner tonight."

"Remind me about it later so I can pretend I can taste the difference." Penelope eyed her husband. "Spit it out. What else did you do this afternoon that you couldn't wait to tell me about?"

"Maybe I just knew that Heidi wanted to run faster?" He dodged her elbow with a laugh. "Brianna called for advice. They got a copy of JP's will today, and Maya was right. He left everything to her."

Penelope groaned. "Tell me she's at least hired her own lawyer."

"She *did*, and Hammerhead had her out of there in less than two hours. Now Purcell is pressuring the coroner to call the death an accident."

"But they can't possibly have the toxicology back yet. Doesn't that take weeks?"

"They'll be lucky to have it back in a couple of months." Jake picked up a child's bicycle blocking the sidewalk, moving it onto the lawn. "It looks bad when a famous artist gets murdered in your town. But a famous artist who picks the wrong plant and puts it in his smoothie isn't the same PR disaster."

Theoretically, the coroner's office was completely independent. In reality, the coroner depended on the support of the police chief to get reelected. Plus, the city council determined budgets, and they would be looking out for the town's reputation.

Having JP's death labeled an accident might be the best thing for Maya. With a will giving her financial motive and her easy access to JP's drink, she was the obvious suspect. But that might leave a murderer walking around town with no one the wiser.

"So what happens now?"

"Now you take Heidi to her home, I go to our house and start trying to find out where Damian's uncle went, and together we'll eventually find out what Brutus ate in the last twenty minutes."

Penelope narrowed her eyes at him and was rewarded by a twitch at the corner of his mouth. "I meant with the investigation into JP's death."

"Oh. Well, the coroner hasn't made a final ruling yet, so Brianna is still investigating. I'll let her know what Max told you. She'll want to talk to him." He paused at the side street that led toward home. "Any special requests for dinner?"

"Surprise me." Penelope leaned in for a quick kiss. "I won't be too late."

EIGHTEEN

Penelope had just administered Grumpy Simon's afternoon insulin when her boss at the post office called. "Do you have time to finish the northeast downtown route?" Roger asked without preamble. "Misty collided with Jonah Peterson's skateboard and broke her leg. I'd do it myself, but my sciatica's acting up."

Eyeing her phone suspiciously, Penelope shook out Grumpy Simon's two allotted post-shot treats. Roger's sciatica was a funny thing. It never reared its head under normal circumstances, but every time he had to deal with irrational staff problems, suddenly no medication could touch the pain. "What's going on?"

"There's nothing..." Roger sighed. "The sorting facility just sent us a batch of damaged letters that got caught up in some machine or something. I don't know. All I know is that they screwed it up, and now I have to deal with angry calls all day. Joe got spooked and said he was going to quit, because one of them is for Mrs. Niedermeyer, and the last time he had to deliver a damaged envelope to her, she threatened him with the evil eye. What are the chances it would happen to her *again*? So Misty offered to take care of his route today, broke her leg, and now half the carriers are taking this as an omen."

None of that was particularly shocking to Penelope. After begging his parents for a skateboard for his thirteenth birthday, Jonah Peterson had spent the next two years attempting to replicate the tricks that would bring him to the attention of the pro circuit. Unfortunately, he had more enthusiasm than talent, though he'd mostly kept the damage to dents and bruises. While the professionals hadn't come calling, Jonah had a large following online who clamored for more videos from "Wipeout Boy." Nobody who loved their car parked it anywhere near the Peterson house.

As for Faith Niedermeyer, she ran a business selling curses and charms from her home, though she was careful to specify everything was for entertainment purposes only. She got more mail than everyone else on the block combined. Statistically, any problem had a good chance of affecting her. And it was even worse because most of the people sending her things included small items in the envelopes for her to work her magic on; legal to mail, yes, but more likely to cause problems with the machines than flat envelopes holding just a sheet or two of paper.

When she had run across an advertisement for Mrs. Niedermeyer's entertainment-purposes-only charms and curses, Penelope had been surprised at the low prices. At that rate, it would take thousands of charms every week just to have enough to cover room and board. Then Jake had pointed out the shipping and handling fee in the small print. With that factored in, the business was likely very profitable.

Mrs. Niedermeyer dealt with every inconvenience by threatening the evil eye. Penelope still wasn't sure what exactly that meant, and she suspected that Mrs. Niedermeyer didn't know either, because Penelope's attempts to clarify things had led to muttering and a slammed door.

All of that put together meant that if Penelope didn't deliver the rest of the mail this afternoon, half the staff would call in sick in the morning, and nobody in town would get their mail delivered. "Fine. Where's the truck?"

"Silvia Peterson has the keys." Roger let out a relieved breath. "You're a lifesaver and I owe you my firstborn."

"Isn't your firstborn turning thirteen this year? No, thanks." Penelope laughed and put Simon's insulin bottle back into the refrigerator. "But you can tell your wife that you tried."

After a quick text to Jake confirmed his willingness to take care of her remaining pet-sitting clients, Penelope jogged four blocks to the Petersons' house. Silvia met her at the door with Misty's mailbag and keys.

When Silvia glanced over her shoulder, Penelope noticed she had three shiny gray strands in her dark brown hair. Silvia looked forward again with a grimace. "Do you want a skateboard?"

"Mom!" The teen's voice coming from within the house made it into two syllables. "I said I was sorry!"

Penelope smiled in sympathy. "It will seem like just a few seconds from now that he's suddenly grown up with his own career."

"Promise?"

Holding up both hands with index and middle fingers crossed, Penelope said, "Absolutely." She held up the keys. "Did Misty say where the truck was parked?" It would be somewhere within a few blocks, but Penelope didn't feel like searching all the alleys.

Silvia pointed to the right. "Just around the corner. Hey,

you want a snickerdoodle? Jonah and I are making a batch to take to Misty in the hospital."

"Only a fool would turn down a snickerdoodle."

With a warm cookie in hand, Penelope picked up where the unfortunate Misty had left off. Mixed in with the rest of the mail were seven clear plastic bags with a long non-apology from the postal service printed on the front, holding the remains of envelopes and letters. Whatever had happened in the sorting center had damaged a lot of mail. Or else they'd been storing it up for some time.

The steady rhythm of walking and delivering mail gave Penelope's thoughts room to run free. Their next trip to the mattress store ought to be the last. Brutus was due for his annual checkup soon. So was Jake, for that matter, but they didn't need a rabies certificate for Jake. When was the last time they'd flushed the water heater? None of the people around JP seemed to have motive *and* opportunity. Could his death really have been an accident? Nobody had said anything about him taking hikes and foraging for food, but then again, Penelope hadn't asked.

Maya would know if JP foraged the ingredients in his smoothies. And Penelope wouldn't even have to manufacture a reason to drop by — one bag with damaged mail had the address of the rented house. It was addressed to "Mr. J. Phi—", which was interesting — it *could* have been meant for "Jean-Philippe Blanchet" and the sender had written it oddly, but it seemed more likely that it was the start of "J. Phillips". As far as Penelope knew, no previous mail had been sent to JP's legal name.

Despite unknowingly causing a potential work stoppage, Mrs. Niedermeyer shrugged as she intercepted Penelope on her way to the front door to deliver the damaged mail. She was wearing a flannel robe and flip-flops. "I tell them to use a padded envelope, but do they? No. They do not."

A nonchalant Faith Niedermeyer was more unnerving than being threatened with the evil eye. Penelope hesitated. "Is everything okay?"

"Wonderful. My grandson was born today. Wait, I have pictures." Reaching into the pocket of her robe, she drew out her phone.

Five minutes later, Penelope extracted herself with the excuse that she needed to deliver the mail. Doting grandmother was a side of Faith Niedermeyer that Penelope had never expected to see, and it was kind of sweet. Four hundred photos was perhaps a bit much, but the woman had never done anything by halves. Perhaps this would usher in a new era for the mail carriers.

At the house JP and Maya had shared, Penelope was delighted to see the driveway empty. Without Ricky Nash around to interfere, she might get more information from Maya. This time, she didn't bother knocking on the front door, but headed down the familiar path to the studio, where Johnny Cash sang about shooting a man just to watch him die. Penelope wondered if the neighbors had complained about the music — the loft doors were closed.

In front of the studio, the pigeon with the fancy feet stood, as if he was just waiting for someone to open the door for him. "Hello, Toes." Penelope scooped him up in one arm so she didn't have to worry about stepping on him, then knocked on the door. "Maya? It's Penelope."

It took longer than Penelope had expected for Maya to open the door, and when she did, she looked terrible. At first, Penelope assumed she'd been drinking again, but there was no smell of alcohol, just a whiff of vomit. Maya rolled the door open wider and stepped back. "You might want to keep your distance. I think I caught the flu from someone at the police station." She rolled the door closed again, shuffled across the room, and threw herself down on the couch.

Toes flew across the room to land on Maya's leg.

Penelope came inside, setting her backpack and mailbag on the floor near the door. "Can I get you anything? Something to drink, maybe?"

Maya groaned. "You don't have any aspirin, do you? My head is killing me."

Digging in her backpack, Penelope found her tiny aspirin bottle and then found a clean-looking mug and filled it with water from the tap next to dozens of drying paintbrushes. "Here you go." She helped Maya sit up, shook two tablets from the bottle, and waited for her to drink. With the practiced ease of someone who had raised a child, she felt Maya's forehead. "Huh. It doesn't *feel* like you're running a fever."

"Can you have the flu without a temperature? It's been so long since I've been sick, I don't even know." She moved Toes onto her shoulder, then drew her legs up and wrapped her arms around them. "Did you hear? JP *did* leave everything to me in his will. Now they really think I had a motive."

Penelope pulled a chair over and sat. "I also heard the police chief is pushing the coroner to call it an accident." The chair was splattered with at least ten layers of paint, and someone had etched a picture of a flying pigeon with feathered ankles into the layers, resulting in technicolor line work. As a work of art, it was lovely, but the chair threatened to collapse when Penelope leaned to the side. "Was JP the type of person to forage for edible plants?"

Maya's eyebrows rose. "JP? Foraging in the vegetable

drawer of the refrigerator was about as much effort as he was willing to put in. And I did most of the shopping."

That confirmed Penelope's belief that JP's death was no accident. But everyone seemed to have an alibi or no motive. She sighed and stood. "Is there a place where you're collecting JP's mail?" The clear plastic bag holding the remains of the envelope was the last piece of mail she needed to deliver. Everything else in the bag was outgoing mail.

"I'll take it into the house the next time I go. There's a stack by the front door. I guess it all goes to... the probate lawyer? Ricky will know." Maya made a move to get up, but sank back. "What is it?"

Penelope squinted to read the rumpled corner of the envelope. "Something from Pitt and Sheehan, LLC. Sounds like lawyers." She handed it over to Maya.

Maya promptly opened the bag. "There's nothing inside the envelope."

"The machine must have eaten it."

Shrugging, Maya put the envelope back inside the bag. "That'll be someone else's problem." She snorted. "What a terrible business name. If I answered phones there, I'd be fired in ten minutes for switching the first syllables."

Penelope took the bag back and stared at it. "Pitt and Sheehan.... Shi — Oh." She laughed. "Jobs answering the phones are the worst, though. If you ever give up painting, you should consider pet sitting. Nobody makes you sign an NDA."

"I should look into that." Maya stared at the envelope again. "JP met some guy named Sheehan at a gallery opening we went to a few months ago. Matt or Mike... something starting with an M, anyhow. They spent half the night talking. I mean, it wasn't unusual for JP to pick up someone at an opening, but I don't think that was what was going on. It didn't look sexual."

"Do you know what they were talking about?"

"No clue. I was busy trying to eat my weight in shrimp cocktail without spilling it on my shirt and watching Ricky check out the other talent. And avoiding Althea. I think I'm allergic to her perfume. I would have skipped the opening completely, but JP had a habit of agreeing to commissions when I wasn't around to stop him."

Maya leaned back, causing Toes to lose his balance. The pigeon flapped to the ground, landing in an ungainly heap before fluffing his feathers and sitting quietly where he'd fallen.

Something about the way the bird was sitting bothered Penelope. "What's wrong with Toes?" In the next second, she was on her feet. "We have to get out of here."

In case of emergency, put on your own oxygen mask first, then assist other passengers. That message had been drilled into Penelope every time she'd been on an airplane, but she was still halfway across the floor to Maya when the meaning sank in. They needed fresh air. Reversing course, she rolled the door all the way open. Then she went back, pulled Maya to her feet and helped her outside, where the artist dropped to the grass.

Penelope made another trip inside the studio to grab Toes before she stopped to call emergency services. "I think there might be a carbon monoxide leak."

NINETEEN

To his credit, Jake waited until they were leaving the emergency veterinarian before he stopped to give Penelope the fierce hug he needed. "I sometimes want to swaddle you in bubble wrap, but you'd probably just jump off a roof to see how well it broke the fall."

When the firefighters had entered the studio with their carbon monoxide meter, a flurry of professional excitement had gone through the entire crew. Apparently, they rarely saw levels that high.

Penelope leaned her forehead against his shoulder. "You'd be glad I did after I spent five hours driving you crazy popping the bubbles." She took a deep breath. "We're almost certainly going to get stuck with the vet bill for keeping Toes in an oxygen cage overnight."

While the paramedics had been willing to stream oxygen toward the pigeon, they'd drawn the line at taking Toes along with Maya to the hospital, mumbling something about pigeons and chlamydia. About the time the ambulance had left, Jake had arrived, so Penelope jumped in the car and they'd sped the pigeon to the emergency veterinarian.

"We can afford it." Jake's arms tightened. "If you hadn't noticed the bird getting sick..."

"The vet told me birds are more sensitive to bad air than people are. That's why they took canaries into coal mines, though Toes is obviously too fancy to go into a mine." She turned to look at him. "And the chlamydia that pigeons have is different from the sexually transmitted disease, so we don't have to worry about that."

The vet had *also* told her that pigeon chlamydia caused flu-like symptoms, though healthy people were unlikely to contract psittacosis. Penelope was glad she hadn't known that earlier, or she might have assumed the pigeon had made Maya sick and left her in the studio to rest. That would certainly have been fatal.

"That hadn't even crossed my mind, but it's good to know." Jake relaxed his hold on her and they began walking back to the car.

Now the danger was over, Penelope found her thoughts spinning. "Do you think Maya's going to be okay? She must have been exposed for a while."

"I got a text while you were signing papers. Jim says they're putting her in a hyperbaric oxygen chamber to be safe, but her symptoms are relatively mild, so she should be discharged in the next day or two."

"Good." After another two steps, Penelope frowned. "Who's Jim?"

"The paramedic who didn't want to get chlamydia."

"Toes saved my life. He deserves a medal."

"When we get home, I'll see if they give medals to pigeons."

Toes would probably look very regal with a medal on a

ribbon around his neck, though it would make flying harder. "Dang it, if we hadn't already told Joann that her painting was genuine, we could add the vet charges to her bill and tell her it was an expense incurred during the investigation."

"Come on. Let's get you home."

The thought of home reminded Penelope of the mail truck. She shook her head. "I have to get the mail back to the post office. And the mailbag is in the studio, so I may need you to schmooze." As the former – and still popular – acting chief of police, Jake knew all the other first responders. They liked and trusted him.

The first responders mostly knew Penelope as well, but in a more "oh no, what happened now" sort of way. Jake could get someone to bring the mailbag out of the studio, even if it was taped off for investigation. If Penelope asked, she'd probably get a lecture about not burning down the building.

Jake's mouth stayed suspiciously straight, almost as if he was biting his cheek in an effort not to smile. He knew exactly why she needed him to do the asking. "I'll see what I can do."

Sitting in the passenger seat as they drove back to the studio, Penelope thought of what she'd learned before Toes had fallen over. "JP got a letter from a law office and I think it was addressed to his legal name."

After braking for a pair of large white geese chasing each other into the street, Jake looked over at her. "To JP or to his estate?"

"The envelope was damaged, so it's hard to say for sure, but if it was about his estate, it should be addressed to 'The estate of' or 'The executors.'" Penelope had delivered enough mail to have seen examples. "This was addressed to him. And it might have been sent before his death. The postmark was missing and whatever was inside the envelope didn't make it."

In the street, the geese honked at each other, and then rushed a car with the temerity to ease past them. Jake sighed and put the car into park as another three geese rushed onto the asphalt to join the fray. "Do you think if we kept pet geese, we could get rid of the roofing salespeople once and for all?"

"I think if we kept pet geese, we'd never get pizza delivered ever again."

"Good point."

A man wearing a t-shirt and shorts got out of his car, making shooing motions to drive the birds to the sidewalk. "Move, you stupid birds!" The honking intensified, from both the geese and the car trapped behind his.

Jake sighed again. "This isn't going to end well."

Penelope patted his shoulder. "Aren't you glad you aren't responsible for handling things like this anymore?"

The lead goose snaked forward and bit the man's bare leg. Penelope put a hand over her mouth to keep from laughing. Having been attacked by territorial geese in the past, she knew they could cause bruises, though they wouldn't inflict any lasting damage on a grown man. But the man in question yelped and ran, leaving his car abandoned in the middle of the lane. Five geese lumbered after him, honking loudly.

"I guess that's one way to deal with geese." Jake put the car in drive and accelerated, passing seven unmoving cars heading the opposite direction. "Do you remember which law firm it was?"

"Uh..." Thinking back from the joke Maya had made, Penelope reconstructed the name. "Pitt and Sheehan? Something like that."

Jake burst out laughing. "That has to be fake."

"If it's not, they need to add a third partner," Penelope agreed. "Preferably someone with a name that teenagers can't make fun of."

Jake shook his head. "There's *no* name teenagers can't make fun of. Trust me. But if I'd had one of those names and set up shop with the other, we would have named it after the area we practiced in. Or something that indicated what kind of law we practiced. Those lawyers are either the most innocent people on the face of the planet, or..." He paused until they had turned onto the street where Maya and JP had lived. "Those lawyers did it on purpose, didn't they?"

"It's pretty effective branding. I *did* remember the name of the law firm."

Pulling in behind the fire chief's car, Jake blew out a breath. "Sometimes I wonder what the world is coming to."

"IT WAS THE WATER HEATER," Jake said as he handed Misty's mailbag to Penelope. "The source of the carbon monoxide," he clarified when he saw her confusion.

"Why would the studio have its own water heater?" A second later, she answered her own question. "Because someone had originally converted it to rent out separately."

"Exactly. And from what they're saying, it wasn't professionally installed, so it was never inspected."

Penelope's own rule was that anything that required turning off water to the house meant a call to a licensed plumber, but some people were more adventurous. "But it's been working all this time. It can't have been that badly installed."

"No, but if the vents were up to code, this couldn't have happened."

They stopped on the sidewalk, the place where they would part ways, Jake to his car and Penelope to the mail truck. "So it really was an accident, then."

Her husband cocked his head, waiting.

Slipping the strap of the mail bag over her head, Penelope tried to look at the big picture. "It's just a little convenient, isn't it? If nobody had come looking for Maya until tomorrow, she probably would have died. And with all the pressure to close the case of JP's death... She wouldn't have been around to defend herself even if the coroner decided it was murder and not an accident. Which it was," she added. "Murder, I mean. Maya said JP wasn't the type to forage for things to add to his smoothies."

"Could have been a mix-up at the grocery store. Sometimes accidents *do* happen. And Maya might have just been unlucky. That's probably been leaking carbon monoxide for a while, but nobody else spent much time in there."

"And she had the hayloft door closed today." At his quizzical look, she pointed at the second floor of the studio. "The other times I've been here, that's been open. It provides pretty good ventilation. Also, it lets Toes get in on his own."

Penelope and Jake stood there, staring at the closed hayloft door. The weather hadn't changed over the past few days, and there'd been no call for rain in the forecast.

Penelope shifted the mailbag on her shoulder. "Why did she close the hayloft doors?"

TWENTY

That evening, lying on the couch with her back against Jake's shoulder, Penelope disconnected her call and put the phone down. "Toes is doing well, and the doctor thinks I can pick him up in the morning."

"Excellent." Jake handed over her plate and unmuted the snooker tournament. They'd ordered pizza for dinner and taken it to the couch, which meant being vigilant. Brutus never took his eye off the prize. Currently, the mastiff was sitting on Penelope's feet, pretending he didn't care about the pizza, but the instant they left food unattended, it would be gone. "Are you just going to take him back to the studio and let him go?"

"I guess. Unless he needs medications every day. Then he might need to live in our spare bedroom for a while." When Jake didn't respond, she turned to look at him. "Not even a sigh?"

"Pigeons are quiet. If you planned to keep a big parrot in there, I'd definitely sigh. Maybe even a couple of times."

Penelope patted his leg and turned back to her pizza. "How's your search for the missing uncle going?"

"It looks like he took the money he stole and drove toward Vegas. I think he changed his name when he ditched the car, so that's going to make things a little harder. But..." He trailed off and waited.

Penelope spoke around a mouthful of pepperoni and sausage. "I know I said it drives me nuts when you hold back information, but that's not the kind of 'drive women crazy' thing those articles are talking about."

Jake snorted. "Fine. The missing uncle is addicted to social media. Ten to one, he's opened up another account and it has at least one post or comment or like linking him back to the old one. I just need to figure out what it is."

"Ooh, a morning of trawling the internet. You live for that sort of thing." Penelope checked in on her son's posts every so often just to keep informed, but she found it hard to get excited about any social media platform. Everyone seemed focused on either pretending their life was always perfect or enraging total strangers to the point they posted regrettable comments. She didn't really need help to shove her foot in her mouth. Besides, her phone's camera left weird splotches on her pictures. The resulting photos were good enough to send to pet owners, but she didn't want to explain what had happened to the lens to strangers around the world.

"You say that, but you don't know how many poker players and coaches this guy follows. It seeps into your brain. At this rate, I'll be running off to Vegas to make my fortune soon."

"Not after I pay the bill for Toes spending the night at the emergency clinic, you won't. They don't coach people at the penny ante tables. Here. Hold this." Handing him her plate, she wiped her fingers and then picked up her laptop. "What was that name again? Oh, right, Pitt and Sheehan.

My bet is they do some sort of probate law. With JP's father dying a few months ago and his grandfather changing his will around, he might have been getting ready to contest something. Or maybe update his own will."

Her posture wasn't ideal for typing accuracy. It took three tries before she found the law firm. "Huh. I wasn't expecting that."

"Hang on." On the television, two balls clicked as they collided, which produced extended clapping from the crowd. Jake piled the plates so he had a free hand to hit the mute button on the remote. "What did you find?"

"Not probate. Intellectual property and contract law."

"Huh."

"That's what *I* said." Penelope took both plates from him so he could retrieve the laptop. At her feet, Brutus raised his head, sniffing the air. "Don't even think about it, buddy." Brutus grumbled and settled down, but cast a sidelong glance to make sure she hadn't put the food somewhere he could reach.

Jake clicked around on the law firm's website, looking at the biographies of both partners, and examining the other posted information. "I thought maybe they had some other types of work they did, but I don't see anything."

"What's Sheehan's first name? Does it start with an M?"

"Hit it in one. Malcolm." Jake set down the laptop and took his plate back, much to Brutus's disappointment. "You want me to get you some tarot cards for your new act as the Amazing Penelope?"

"I'm always amazing. You know that." She took another bite. "Maya said JP was talking to someone named Sheehan at some gallery opening. I think it must be him. But why would JP be talking to someone about intellectual property rights when Ricky Nash takes care of all their licensing?"

"Maybe he didn't want Nash to handle the licensing anymore."

"They didn't have a choice." Penelope slumped against her husband and ate another bite in frustration. "The NDA meant they couldn't even talk to anyone about it. From the thirty seconds I've spent in his presence, Ricky Nash doesn't seem like someone who would give idle threats. Even *talking* to a lawyer would probably let that guy take their earnings. At least, Maya thought it would. JP must have known that." She tapped the crust against her plate. "I wish we could find out what was in that envelope. For all we know, it was torrid poetry. Maya said their relationship didn't look sexual, but maybe she was wrong."

"I'll mention it to Brianna. She might be able to get Sheehan to give her some idea of what he sent. Unless it was a love letter, of course, but most lawyers would be smart enough not to send that using official stationery."

"It would save them the cost of a stamp," Penelope pointed out.

"Lawyers in big firms don't open their own mail. If it got returned as undeliverable..."

"You're probably right," Penelope admitted. "Besides, I think everyone does that sort of thing over the internet these days, anyhow. Why wait a week to get a response when you can get a naked selfie in minutes?" She thought about that as she chewed. "It does take the romance out of it, though."

"I think I can promise I'll never send you a naked selfie."

"That's because you're a romantic guy." Penelope shifted so she could lay her head on his shoulder.

"Exactly." He hit the button on the remote, letting the sounds of the snooker tournament fill the room.

Penelope snorted and changed the subject. "When do you want to go back to the mattress store?"

"I never *want* to go there again, but tomorrow morning is free apart from looking at poker players. Are you sure you don't want to get that one we were looking at?"

"I'm not sleeping on a bed that's spying on me. Can you imagine what it would think when Brutus jumped on the bed?"

"It would think he's a very good boy." Jake tossed the dog a slice of pepperoni, and it disappeared in a quick chomp.

Penelope elbowed him lightly. "Don't give him that. Pepperoni's bad for him."

"But it's good for us?" Jake leaned forward to pick up the box. "Another slice?"

"Tomorrow we're going to have a salad."

"Absolutely." As he dropped another slice on her plate, Jake kissed her forehead. "We'll pick one up on the way back from the mattress store."

TWENTY-ONE

But their plans to go shopping for a mattress yet again had to be postponed when Maya called Penelope in the morning. "I know you don't really know me, but is there any way you could give me a ride home from the hospital? Ricky was making such a fuss over me that I told him I already had a ride, so if I show up in a taxi now..."

Penelope picked up the slobbery tennis ball at her feet and tossed it halfway across the dog park, watching Rocco for any signs he was getting tired. "Not a problem. I have a couple things I need to do first — if I show up in an hour or so, would that work? I can send Jake if you want to leave earlier."

"Thank you so much. An hour is fine. It will probably take me that long to sign all the forms."

"See you then." Rocco came running back and dropped the ball at her feet again, his bright pink tongue hanging from his mouth. He was a black lab, with just a hint of silver around his muzzle, and he was convinced he had the stamina of a young dog. After throwing the ball again, she texted her husband. *Need to reschedule the mattress shopping. Going to pick up Maya.*

Ten seconds later, her phone vibrated. *Not sure how I will survive the disappointment. Love you.* She grinned.

If Maya was feeling up to it, they would pick up Toes on the way home. The veterinarian had called to let her know the pigeon was stable and no longer needed oxygen. The more time they spent driving around together, the more time Penelope would have to ask about JP. And she still wanted to know how the studio's hayloft doors had ended up closed.

Rocco's dash back ended in a belly flop on the grass in front of her. "Good timing!" She picked up the ball and put it in her pocket. "Let's let you catch your breath and then we'll walk home. I have to ask an artist a bunch of questions."

MAYA WAS WAITING in the hospital lobby, barefoot aside from the hospital-issued socks with non-slip soles, when Penelope arrived. She jumped up from the hard plastic chair. "Thank you so much for coming to pick me up." Before Penelope had a chance to respond, Maya had taken her arm and turned her so they were going outside. In a lower voice, she said, "I'm pretty sure Ricky is somewhere in the hospital looking for me, and I really don't have the energy to deal with him right now. Do you mind?"

Penelope loved a good evasion, especially when it was someone she, too, was trying to avoid. "Can you walk to the visitors' parking lot, or do you want to hide out in the bathroom until I bring the car up?"

"I can walk." Maya let Penelope guide her through the

wide automatic doors and to the right, down the sidewalk and across the asphalt to the visitors' parking. "The doctor said I shouldn't do any strenuous exercise for a few days and to come back if I feel short of breath." She looked at Penelope. "Did I ever thank you for saving my life? You must be my fairy godmother or something."

"You're welcome." Holding open the passenger door, Penelope chanced a look at the building. An irritated Ricky Nash shaded his eyes with one hand as he scanned the area. "Let's get out of here before he looks this way."

Maya dove into the car. Penelope scooted to the other side, not daring to look to see if Ricky had noticed them. Then she backed out carefully and took the long way out of the parking lot to avoid being seen. In her rear view mirror, Ricky was still looking around. "I don't think he saw us."

Maya leaned back in her seat. "Thank you again. I know I should be grateful to him for all he's done for my career, but sometimes he's hard to be around."

It seemed to Penelope that Ricky had benefited far more from Maya's work than the other way around. "I thought maybe he'd left town. His car wasn't in the driveway when I came to see you yesterday."

"Yeah, he and Althea were on a plane, going to a showing for another client, when they heard about what happened. When it landed, they hopped on another plane to come right back." Maya slumped in her seat. "Ugh. I feel like such a horrible person for sneaking out like that, but he just talks non-stop, and when he's not talking to me, he's on the phone talking to someone else, and sometimes I just need... silence. Or maybe not silence, because I always have the music on, but I can tune that out."

"I get it. That's why dogs and cats are so much easier to be around than people."

"Exactly!" Maya sat up straighter and moved the seat belt so it wasn't cutting into her neck. "It was easier when JP was around, because he would walk off while he and Ricky were talking. Ricky would follow him, and I could work in peace."

At the light where she would have turned left to go to the studio, Penelope turned right. "You don't mind a quick detour, do you?"

"That's fine. My doctors weren't super happy about me being around paint for a few days anyhow. I don't know what I'm going to do with myself."

They drove in silence for ten minutes, and Penelope wasn't too surprised to hear gentle snores coming from the passenger seat. Sleeping in a hospital was never easy, and Maya was still recovering. After Penelope pulled the car into a shaded spot in the lot, she rolled all the windows down and woke Maya just enough to tell her she'd be right back. Maya was asleep again before she even made it out of the car.

Though Penelope had taken many animals home from the animal hospital, they'd all been pets, belonging to her or a client. Picking up a pigeon that nobody actually owned was a novel experience. After she'd settled the bill with the receptionists, she was placed in a small exam room so a vet tech could go over the discharge instructions with her.

Apparently, the evening staff hadn't communicated Toes's footloose and fancy free status to the morning staff. The vet tech, a pale woman with blue hair and splotchy tattoos covering both forearms, came in with a stack of handouts and pamphlets. "Most of this you won't need to worry about for the moment, but I've got info on proper diet and good coop designs that can be easily disinfected. Also, a pamphlet on the risks of psittacosis in humans, in case you have anyone in the household who is immunocompromised."

Normally, Penelope would have let the younger woman talk — most of the information looked interesting, and she never knew what weird tidbits she might pick up from other people. Plus, she was trying to figure out what the tattoo on the woman's wrist was meant to be. It might have been a rabbit, or maybe it was a duck and what looked like ears were actually the bill. The lines were thick, in a way that Penelope associated with tattoos created by amateurs.

But today, Penelope didn't want to leave Maya unattended in the car for too long. "Toes is a wild pigeon, or at least he just lives in the neighborhood as far as I know. I don't think we can fix his diet if people drop French fries nearby. But I'll pass all this along to Maya, in case she decides to adopt him."

"Oh. He has the fancy feet, so we all just assumed he was a pet or a show pigeon." The vet tech still looked confused, even as she handed the pamphlets to Penelope. "Didn't he come in for carbon monoxide poisoning? Did he get stuck in a garage with the car running or something?"

"No, he came into the artist's studio where there was a carbon monoxide build-up. If he hadn't been there, she might have died."

The vet tech blinked. "That's amazing. Though it would have been a lot cheaper to buy a carbon monoxide alarm."

Penelope couldn't help the laugh that came out. "You're absolutely right."

"Okay, so the discharge instructions are pretty simple. Keep an eye on Toes for the next few days. If he's not eating or drinking normally, or if he seems to have trouble breathing, he needs to come back in. Any questions? If not, I'll get Mr. Toes for you."

A few minutes later, Penelope was back at the car carrying a confused-looking Toes. In the passenger seat, Maya looked at her ringing phone as if it were a venomous snake. *Ricky* flashed on the screen. Penelope slid into the driver's seat, leaned over and pushed the red button to send the call to voicemail. "You can call him back when you're ready. In the meantime, I have a surprise for you." She passed the carrier over.

Maya's eyes watered. "Toes!" She looked at Penelope. "I was afraid to ask what had happened to him. I thought he'd died."

Inside the carrier, Toes cooed and leaned into Maya's fingers, though he still looked confused.

Maya's phone rang again, and this time she was the one to hit the red button.

Penelope handed over the discharge instructions and the handful of pamphlets. "I know he's a wild bird... sort of... but the vet wants us to keep an eye on him for a few days. You can borrow this crate if you want to keep him at your place, and we can stop by the pet store to get some food, or I can keep him at my place, if that works better."

Maya looked up from murmuring to Toes. "Ricky and Althea are staying at the house, and she has this *thing* about birds. You don't mind keeping Toes for a few days?"

"Not a problem." Penelope started the car and backed out of the spot, trying to decide if there was a subtle way to find out what she wanted to know. Finally, she decided to just ask. "Why were the hayloft doors on the studio closed yesterday?"

"Hm? Oh, you mean the shutters on the second floor?" At Penelope's nod, Maya sighed. "Althea probably started it, but Ricky complained about Toes coming in and all the dust getting on the canvases. He was going on and on about how he needed a bunch of new paintings now so he could add them to the inventory of what 'Jean-Philippe' had created before he died. I told him to close those shutters just to make him stop talking and go away." She sighed again. "That's part of why he's being so annoying now. He feels really guilty that having those shutters closed nearly killed me. How many times can someone apologize before it's irritating?"

About to pull out onto the road, Penelope stopped the car. A little voice inside her head told her that taking Maya home was a bad idea. Penelope had spent half a century learning to ignore that voice, figuring she'd find a way out of whatever predicament she'd gotten herself into. But this wasn't about her. This was about Maya. "Do you feel like coming to stay at my house with Toes for a few days? It's just me and my husband and our dog, so it's pretty quiet."

"Your husband won't mind?"

"No. I already told him Toes might be staying with us." Maya might be louder than a pigeon, especially if she turned up the music, but she'd probably still be quieter than a parrot. And Jake would understand if Penelope told him she was worried about Maya's safety.

"Ricky's going to have a cow."

"Text him and tell him you're staying with a friend. But don't say who." Penelope didn't want Ricky Nash showing up at her front door and bullying Maya into going back to her studio to paint while he talked at her until she agreed to whatever new scheme he had cooked up.

It was possible Ricky would figure it out on his own — Maya didn't know many people in town, and Penelope had a fairly distinct and memorable name. Everybody knew where she lived. But Penelope had no problem harnessing the accidental damage of Brutus to keep unwanted visitors away. And if Brutus didn't work, there was always Jake.

"I want to stay with you," Maya said firmly. "But I might need to borrow some clothes unless I can sneak into the house while Ricky's out." On her lap, Toes cooed his agreement and pecked at the side of the carrier.

TWENTY-TWO

They'd driven by the rental house without slowing, to see if Ricky's car was in the driveway, and then parked around the corner, climbed over the back fence, and went into the house. The studio door was covered with crime scene tape, which Penelope hadn't expected. Maya threw a random assortment of clothes into a paper bag, grabbed her purse, and scuttled down the stairs again. It was clear she really didn't want to be there when Ricky returned.

To his credit, Jake didn't bat an eyelash when Penelope walked through the door with Maya and Toes. "Nice to meet you," he said when Penelope introduced him to Maya. "Not many pigeons come with their own personal assistant."

Maya smiled at the floor.

Penelope blew him a kiss behind Maya's back as she guided the artist to the guest bedroom. When Penelope had called Jake from the driveway to ask that he put Brutus in his crate, he hadn't asked any questions. Though Toes didn't seem to be bothered by much, Penelope didn't want to stress the pigeon out by having the mastiff excitedly sniffing at the carrier. Birds were fragile, even at the best of times.

"Let me get you and Toes settled in, and then I'll introduce you to Brutus."

While Maya was unpacking, Penelope went out to the kitchen to hug her husband. "I got a bad feeling about having her stay at that house," she said, by way of explanation. "Maya, not Toes," she added. "Though maybe Toes, too. Ricky seems to have it in for pigeons." After another pause, she said, "I know he doesn't have a motive for murdering JP, so it's not that. It's that he's putting undue pressure on Maya. Plus the whole hating pigeons thing."

Used to Penelope's non-linear conversational flow, Jake nodded. "Then it's good they're staying here."

A muffled *woof* came from the office, a gentle reminder from Brutus that he was locked up in another room when interesting things were happening and he was sad about it.

"I knew there was a reason I married you, despite the lumpy mattress." Penelope kissed him. "How goes the search for the missing uncle? Have you learned any good poker tips yet?"

Jake's lips twitched. "It's important to memorize the different hands."

"One time!" Penelope tapped his chest with her index finger. "It was *one* time." Back when they had first started dating, Penelope agreed to sit in for him for a hand during a friendly low-stakes poker game at his house while he spoke to the desk sergeant about a problem. In the fifteen minutes he'd been gone, the rest of the table had picked up on her repeated glances at the rank card. Jake had come back to a significantly smaller stack of poker chips than he'd had when he left.

Penelope's excuse was that she didn't enjoy sitting around playing cards when she could be doing almost anything else. She would never be good at it and she didn't like it, so why spend time memorizing hands when she'd never use that knowledge? After that evening, she'd made sure she had pet-sitting jobs to keep her busy when Jake hosted the poker game.

He trapped her hand against his chest. "Honestly, I haven't been watching the videos or reading the advice. I've just been going through the people reacting to each post and checking how long their accounts have been around. My short list has five people. Hopefully, I'll be able to tell if one of them is my missing man."

"Should be easy enough. Look for the one who's not posting selfies. If he's really trying to hide his identity, you can get him by what he's *not* saying," she said, raising her eyebrows and nodding. "Just like that Sherlock Holmes story about the dog that didn't bark." It was the only Arthur Conan Doyle tale she remembered; the rest she'd ignored as nineteenth-century versions of Hollywood-esque CSI, where evidence was present, unambiguous, and always accurate. Those sorts of television shows drove Jake up the wall.

"In this variation, am I Sherlock Holmes or Watson?"

"You're the dog." Penelope turned to smile at Maya, who had come out of the bedroom, closing the door behind her. "Right. Let's introduce you to Brutus."

It took a good five minutes for Brutus to finish sniffing Maya, likely a combination of hospital, painting, and pigeon smells. Eventually, he agreed to stop following Maya around and lie on the couch in the living room with a frozen treat. Maya settled in next to him with a book, looking ready to fall asleep again.

"Ricky's probably going to show up at some point," Penelope said to her husband in a low voice. "He called seven times while we were driving home. Don't let him railroad her into agreeing to go anywhere with him."

"I'll be polite, yet firm."

"Excellent." She'd seen Jake at his most icily polite. Even Ricky Nash would be no match for him. "I have to go take care of some animals." She slung her backpack over one shoulder, then stopped. "Why would the studio have police tape blocking the door? I thought they already figured out the water heater caused the problem."

Cocking his head, Jake frowned. "That... sounds like something else is going on." He held up a hand to forestall her excited questions. "I'll ask. It may be nothing more than fire and police department territorial squabbling."

"But it *could* be something else."

Jake looked over at the couch. "Maybe the fewer people who know where she is, the better."

TWENTY-THREE

Penelope stood in Laura Wilmot's backyard and surveyed the damage. All but one of the terracotta pots lining the walkway had been knocked over, a hole had been dug in the lawn, and the outdoor furniture was scattered around the yard.

Putting her hands on her hips, she shook her head. "Yes. I'm a little late with your breakfast, but surely that wasn't worth all *this*."

The culprit stood on the walkway and blinked at her. Speedy, a forty-year-old African spurred tortoise, took two steps and used his seventy-pound bulk to shove the chair another foot to the side.

"You had hay and grass," Penelope pointed out. She crouched to rub his carapace, brushing off a smear of dirt. "Your mom is going to think someone broke into the yard."

Speedy's owner would think no such thing. In fact, she'd warned Penelope that the tortoise would likely spend most of the three days she was gone destroying things. "He seems to enjoy knocking things around, so I drag everything back where it belongs every day to give him something to do. I have more pots in the garage if he breaks them."

Still shaking her head, Penelope went back inside the house to get Speedy's lettuce and fruit, locking the sliding glass door behind her so the tortoise didn't follow. Laura had warned her about that, too. "When he gets inside, he does a lot of damage." Scrapes near the baseboards and ripped sections of carpet bolstered her story. "It took me a while to realize he can open the sliding door unless it's locked."

Laura had inherited the destructive reptile from her parents, and she provided for him in her own will. "Some people divide their assets among their children. I have a will to provide for the wrecking ball on four legs," she'd laughed. "He's going to outlast us all."

For Penelope, the responsibility of a huge tortoise was still a better inheritance than all of JP's grandfather's money. She mulled over the reasons JP would have contacted an intellectual property and contracts lawyer while she rinsed mustard and dandelion greens and a strawberry. Technically, the tortoise wasn't supposed to get any fruit at all, but the owner's parents had given him one strawberry every day. Since it hadn't hurt him in forty years, Laura observed the ritual at Speedy's current home.

The obvious answer was that JP was looking for a way out of playing the role of Jean-Philippe Blanchet. That fit with everything else she'd heard of his recent behavior — the trade school brochures hidden in his room and the fight with Maya. What had seemed like a great idea when he and Maya had first signed quickly became stifling. But had he just reached his breaking point and decided to accept the consequences of terminating the agreement, or was there something else going on?

She sighed, piling the food into a stainless steel bowl

and adding a handful of fig leaves from a container in the fridge. If only she could get a look at the contents of the damaged envelope. But either the letter had been damaged beyond any chance of piecing together, or it had been separated from the envelope and it wasn't clear who the recipient should be. Probably the former, since the lawyer's signature block would have had the firm's name.

Speedy knocking his bulk against the glass distracted her. "I'm almost ready," she called. "Keep your shell on." While she shredded a carrot, she considered what else JP could have asked the lawyer to do. He'd had a will already, so it was unlikely he'd have asked a firm that didn't do estate planning to make revisions. The only occasions Penelope had needed lawyers were for her divorce from Seth's father and the times she'd been arrested. She had a vague idea of other types of law, but no real specifics.

A harder knock against the glass told her she'd better stop thinking and get Speedy his meal. "Relax! If you break the glass, I'll have to explain it to my insurance people and I'm still trying to live down our *last* conversation." Grabbing the bowl, she hurried through the door, twice nearly tripping on Speedy as she stashed the contents in multiple places in the yard. Anyone who thought tortoises were slow had never seen Speedy trying to find the strawberry.

The tangling thoughts of insurance, damage, and JP's relationship with a contracts attorney unrolled into a new idea. Penelope poked at it as she opened the shed to get more hay. JP and Maya hadn't been willing to do anything that might violate the NDA and bring on the wrath of Ricky Nash because doing so would bankrupt them both.

But that threat lost its teeth if JP inherited money — real money — from his grandfather. JP would be able to afford the NDA penalties, and with a good lawyer might avoid even that. True, JP didn't have the money yet, but if he had a good chance of one day inheriting, someone might gamble on a loan.

Speedy bumped into her calves as he took his victory lap around the yard, his mouth stained red with strawberry juice. "That's still not motive for murder, though, is it?" she asked the tortoise as she scratched his shell. "Killing JP ruins the Jean-Philippe brand. Even if Maya keeps creating Blanchet works, how many extra paintings can you really say you had in storage before people get suspicious?" She gave the tortoise one last pat. "I don't like Ricky because of the way he acts around Maya, but that doesn't make him a killer."

With a grunt, Speedy crashed into the last pot, knocking it over. The rim crunched as it hit the walkway, and dirt spilled everywhere.

Penelope shook her head as she picked up the large clay shards. "It's a good thing you aren't on my suspect list. You wouldn't hesitate a moment, would you?"

The tortoise flipped potting soil onto her shoe in agreement.

TWENTY-FOUR

After working quickly to catch up, Penelope went home for a late lunch. Jake had sent her one text in the past hour. *Brutus is in love.*

Penelope assumed Brutus had found a new best friend in Maya, but it was within the realm of possibility that the mastiff had fixated on Toes. Their dog sometimes surprised her.

The first thing she heard when she opened the door was a contented coo from the guest bedroom. "Hello, Toes!" Then she found Jake in the kitchen, carefully constructing three sandwiches. Two were peanut butter and banana, and the third was peanut butter and honey. "I take it Maya and Brutus are somewhere together?"

"In the backyard. Painting." He cut one sandwich into two rectangles, another sandwich — this one with the crusts cut off — diagonally into triangles, and paused at the third. "Weird cut or normal cut? She *is* an artist, but she seems reasonably sensible."

"Don't pretend your diagonal sandwich nonsense is normal." Opening the refrigerator, Penelope looked at the vegetable drawer. "Weren't we going to have a salad today?"

"We have a guest."

Penelope flashed him a grin, then took out the baby carrots and a browning head of broccoli. "I don't think I can save this." She dumped it in the food waste bucket, carefully locking the lid afterward, and returned to the fridge, only then noticing what had been stuck to it with a magnet advertising the local pharmacy.

On a sheet of printer paper, someone had immortalized Brutus's paw print in orange paint and then drawn blurry mastiffs jumping and playing around and behind it. A perfect replica of Toes stood in the bottom corner, pecking at seeds. "That's adorable!" Penelope leaned closer to look at the details, then stepped back. "Did you take her to buy art supplies?"

"She used the leftover tempera paint in the garage."

They looked at each other for a long moment. Finally, Penelope said, "Wasn't that all dried up?" She'd last used it to create posters to cheer on one of Esther's friends who was running a marathon, but that had been a few years ago.

"It can't have been," Jake said slowly, "because if it *was* dried out, you would have thrown it away the last time we cleaned out that cupboard in the garage."

"Right. Of course." Penelope cleared her throat. They'd had a long *discussion* about her need to keep things that were no longer good and his need to get rid of stuff that they might need again. In the end, she'd promised to clean out the cupboard, and he'd promised not to judge her choice of what to keep. "Obviously, they *weren't* dried out or Maya wouldn't have been able to use them."

"She mixed them with water and shook them for thirty minutes."

Penelope gestured at the picture tacked to the fridge with the bag of carrots. "See? Aren't you glad we didn't throw them away? We got a Jean-Philippe Blanchet original out of the deal." She frowned. "Maybe we should move it someplace else so it doesn't get wrinkled. Or eaten. This might be what I have to borrow against to keep you in the nicer old folks' home before I run off with the rest of the money."

"Maya said if something happens to it, she'll make us another one. But she said she's not signing anything as Blanchet anymore."

Penelope's eyes widened. "Ooh, Ricky's going to have a conniption fit when he hears that. I think he was planning on riding that train for as long as he could." She waited until Jake had placed the sandwiches on plates, then brushed the crumbs off the cutting board and started slicing apples. "Did you find out why the crime scene tape is still on the studio?"

Jake leaned against the counter and watched her. "I did. Remember how I said the water heater hadn't been installed by a professional?"

"Yes."

"Turns out, that's not why the carbon monoxide built up. Someone had crammed a paper bag with a bunch of those packing peanuts made from cornstarch into the duct."

Penelope set down the paring knife so she didn't cut herself. "What?"

"Definitely not an accident."

"That's no good. Have you told Maya?"

"Not yet. I figure she's safe enough in our backyard at the moment."

"I'm glad she's staying here." Two attempted murders meant to look like accidents; one had succeeded and one hadn't. But were they two attempts to murder the same person? Had Maya been the target of the second attempt, or was it JP? "How long was it there? Could they tell?"

"Best guess, sometime between one day and one week."

"Ugh." That didn't help at all. A week ago, JP had been alive — he could have been the intended victim. When that plan hadn't worked, the killer might have switched tactics and poisoned his smoothie. If the duct had been blocked *after* JP's death, Maya had to have been the target. "If it was a week ago, wouldn't they have removed the bag after JP's death? Why take a chance that someone else might die?"

"Access? The detectives were there for the next couple of days. Maybe the killer had to leave town or just didn't want to risk getting caught. They might not have realized the loft doors were open all the time and just assumed it didn't work."

"Or Maya really *was* the target." Penelope went back to slicing apples. "If she was, that changes things. Who would want to get rid of both JP *and* Maya?"

Two seconds after the door to the backyard opened, Brutus bounded into the kitchen, splotches of color on his fur. Maya followed more slowly. "Sorry about all the paint. He kept trying to play. I'll clean his fur after I wash up." She came to a halt in the kitchen entrance. "You both look so serious. What happened?"

Penelope blocked Brutus's sniffing nose with one hand, gave him an apple slice, and pointed at his bed in the corner of the kitchen. "It looks like the carbon monoxide poisoning wasn't an accident. Someone sabotaged the studio."

"Oh." Maya looked between them, then down at her hands. "Huh." With no change of expression, she added, "I need to clean up." She turned on her heel and went into the bathroom.

Jake raised his eyebrows and tilted his head. "That went... better than I thought it would."

Remembering how Maya always seemed to hide in the studio when people were around, Penelope hummed. "I think this is a 'silent waters run deep' situation."

"I guess I've grown used to more shallow, louder waters."

Penelope stuck out her tongue at him. "You knew what you were signing up for."

Leaning in to kiss her, Jake smiled. "I certainly did."

TWENTY-FIVE

By the next morning, it was clear that adding a third person to the household required a trip to the grocery store. Not because they didn't have enough food at home, but because Penelope wouldn't inflict her usual random meals on someone who might be too polite to scrape their plate into Brutus's bowl and order takeout when the entrée was inedible.

Maya had jumped at the chance to go along to the store. Though the artist claimed she wanted to get a notebook, Penelope suspected she just wanted to get out of the house.

As far as food went, Maya was even less exacting than Penelope and Jake. "I usually just eat the same thing for a few weeks at a time. Then I get sick of it and eat something else. So if we get more bread and peanut butter, I'll be set."

That explained the fast food bags in the studio's garbage. Penelope added two bags of salad greens to the cart, positioning them to hide the crackers and cheese spread. "Who would want to harm both you and JP?"

"I don't know. We lived almost completely separate lives, even though we shared the house. The only thing we really had in common was the art. And nobody kills anyone else over art." Picking up a dragon fruit, she stared at it. "Half my friends in art school *tried* to offend people, and everyone just yawned." She put the dragon fruit down again.

"You and JP didn't have friends or enemies in common? Maybe someone who was jealous?" They had a container of hummus in the refrigerator, but was it still good? Did hummus even go bad? Penelope grabbed another container, just in case.

"JP got along with everyone. I don't go out enough to make any enemies."

Candied almonds would be good on a salad. She might as well get the large container so they could snack on them. "Ex-boyfriends or ex-girlfriends?"

"Ugh. I've given up. The last guy I went out with — this was years ago, before I met JP — this guy and I hit it off right away. Three months later, he brought his wife to an exhibition."

"Oof."

"I had to pretend we were just acquaintances. And then, when I refused to see him again, he had the nerve to tell me it was my fault for falling into the 'bourgeois trap of monogamy.' He kept bugging me until I threatened to tell his wife. And then other people found out and everyone in our local scene was laughing about it for the next six months."

"That explains it." At Maya's questioning look, Penelope said with a grimace, "Althea Nash made some comment about how I should protect Jake from you."

"How did she...? Ugh. That story's going to haunt me for the rest of my life." Maya rolled her eyes. "Can you imagine?

Me as a femme fatale? Ridiculous. I don't know how JP did it."

It occurred to Penelope that Maya's partner was a more likely candidate. "JP and Ricky never...?"

"As far as I know, Ricky's straight. Besides, he has a type. His first wife was an actress on a soap opera. Althea modeled in Europe before she became a publicist. And Ricky's always willing to spend a little extra time at galleries with the female artists who just happen to be tall and thin, even if they're already represented."

"I can't say I'm surprised."

Maya shrugged. "They're welcome to him. Who needs men when you can build colonies with your friends online?"

Penelope opened her mouth to rebut that premise, then decided she'd have to spend some time formulating her answer and changed the topic. "What do you like to drink?"

Within fifteen minutes, they had filled the cart with a mixture of very healthy food and also food Penelope actually wanted to eat, plus a few frozen meals that straddled the divide. It was only when they were waiting in the checkout line that a thought occurred to Penelope. "You know those smoothies that JP drank? Did you ever drink them, too?"

"For a couple of weeks. JP was trying to convince me to eat healthier, so he tried a bunch of different flavors. I really liked the spicy mint ones." She shrugged one shoulder. "It was like everything else, though. After a couple of weeks, I couldn't stand them anymore and I switched to mushroom and pineapple pizza. After that, it was meatball subs, and then after that, it was orange chicken with zucchini from the panda restaurant."

Penelope hoped Maya's doctor occasionally tested her for vitamin deficiencies, but that was a conversation for a later date. They piled all the food onto the conveyor belt, along with two notebooks and a pack of colored pencils.

Using the excuse of the line behind them to take a raincheck on getting updates on the cashier's grandchildren, Penelope piled the purchases into bags as she considered what Maya had said.

Everyone had assumed JP had been the intended victim of the poisoned smoothie, but what if Maya had been the target all along?

TWENTY-SIX

When they arrived back at Penelope and Jake's house, the red convertible was parked in front. Maya slid down in the passenger seat as they drove closer. "Maybe you could drop me off around the block and I'll take a walk until the coast is clear."

Leaving Maya wandering around on her own seemed like a terrible idea if someone had already tried to kill her twice. "Ricky and Althea aren't dog people, are they?" At Maya's head shake, Penelope pulled into the driveway. "If you don't mind staying outside with Brutus, you should be safe."

As she'd expected, Brutus had been exiled to the yard. When Penelope opened the side gate, the mastiff trotted around the side of the house to investigate, saw Maya, and immediately went into a play bow. "Avoid the windows," Penelope cautioned, then closed the gate and grabbed the bags of groceries and went through the front door. "Jake, I'm home!"

Her husband came out of the kitchen, head slightly

tilted in an unspoken question, with Ricky on his heels. "You've met the Nashes."

"Of course." Penelope smiled at Ricky as she passed him, and then again at Althea, who was seated at the table with a mug of coffee. "How are you both?"

But Ricky was still staring at the door. "Where's Maya? I have some papers for her to sign."

Althea shook her head. "Forgive my husband. He doesn't understand that not everyone is trying to close deals all day, every day."

"She said she had some errands to run," Penelope offered. "Do you want me to give her a message for you? If you leave the papers here, I'll make sure she gets them."

"Why isn't she responding to my texts?" Ricky demanded.

Because she doesn't want to talk to you, Penelope thought, but she didn't say it. "She's been working on getting healthy. I'm sure she'll get back to you soon. Are you staying in town long?"

"I need to catalog the artwork in the studio, and Maya..." He flung one arm out instead of finishing the sentence, leaving Penelope wondering how he'd planned to end it. *Maya knows which paintings are finished? Maya could hurry up and paint more and we'll be able to call them Jean-Philippe Blanchet works?* But Ricky couldn't say either of those to Penelope and Jake, because, as far as he knew, they still believed JP had been the artist behind the name.

From the spare bedroom came a tentative cooing, as Toes heard Penelope putting groceries away. Althea abruptly set down her coffee cup and stood. "Ricky, she's not here. Just leave the contracts for her to send later. Let's go."

Ricky looked from Penelope to Jake with suspicion, as if ready to catch any hint of deception, but Penelope maintained a bland smile and Jake merely loomed pleasantly. "Fine. But tell her to call me!"

"Of course," Jake said. He saw them to the door while Penelope finished stowing the frozen food. When the door closed and he returned, he said, "I thought they were planning on camping out until Maya showed up, and then they rushed off. What happened?"

"Ornithophobia," Penelope said, having looked up the proper term earlier. "Althea's freaked out by birds."

"Ah." Jake glanced toward the slider to the backyard. "I take it Maya is in the yard and that's the reason Brutus stopped leaning his head against the door?"

"It seemed safer than letting her walk around unprotected." She relayed the information she'd gleaned from Maya about the smoothies and then brought up her new theory, that Maya had been the target all along. "Though that would mean JP's inheritance had nothing to do with any of this, which seems like a lot of wasted effort on my part." She frowned. "And I can't think of any reason anyone would want to hurt Maya."

"So you've exchanged motive for opportunity." Jake eyed the bag he was unloading. "Are we hoarding hummus for some reason? I only ask because we now have three unopened containers."

"You never know when you might need more." Penelope handed him the last bag to put away. "I'm going to let Maya know it's safe to come inside."

TWENTY-SEVEN

Two days after the hospital had discharged her, Maya had run out of art supplies and Toes was ready to be released. Penelope and Maya were lingering over a late lunch, the crumbs from two peanut butter and honey sandwiches in front of them, while Brutus slept in the kitchen corner. Maya had taught the mastiff to hold a paintbrush in his jaws and turn his head to create streaks on paper. Then she took those streaks and turned them into mischievous sprites with a few quick dabs. Penelope had watched her do it multiple times, and still couldn't see how she went from a swipe of paint to a tableau of creatures with expressions and movement. It was magic.

It was also completely different from Jean-Philippe's style, making Penelope wonder what Maya's future held. Maya seemed content not to worry about it for the moment.

Since the Nashes had gone to the capital for the day — Ricky had finally realized repeatedly calling wasn't doing anything, so he had switched to texting, offering to bring Maya along to events and promising not to pressure her — and nobody else knew where Maya was staying other than

Esther, Jake had felt comfortable leaving Maya at the house while he went to talk to his clients. The missing uncle had indeed been using an alternate social media account; his reflection was visible in more than one photo. From there, it had taken less than five minutes to determine the city and hotel. Now, it was up to the clients to decide how they wanted to handle things. Jake needed to talk them through their options, though he'd promised to be back in time to go back to the mattress store.

"Should we take him back to the studio to release him?" Maya poked her finger into the carrier to scratch the pigeon's head. "Or would it be okay if I just let him go in your backyard?"

Toes cooed in his normal, slightly confused manner, the sound making Brutus's ear twitch, though his snores didn't abate.

"I don't know." Pigeons flew all over the town, so surely Toes would be able to navigate back to his preferred spot. But then again, Penelope had never seen Toes do anything besides testing the paper towel lining the carrier to see if it was edible. And he pecked at *that* every few minutes. It was possible Toes was not the sharpest tool in the shed. "Maybe he should go back to the studio." At least he was pretty.

"Okay." Maya took both plates to the sink, tossing a crust to Brutus along the way. Though the mastiff had seemed deeply asleep half a second before, he lifted his head in time to snatch it from the air. "Do you want to go along?"

"Of course."

After a brief discussion, they elected to leave Brutus at home. Penelope claimed it was because he'd already had his long walk of the day with Jake, but really she didn't trust him not to reflexively grab Toes if the pigeon fluttered too near. For the mastiff, other dogs were usually friends, cats were terrifying, and squirrels were fun to chase. Penelope didn't know what category pigeons fell into.

If Toes had been bred with better survival instincts, Penelope would have trusted the pigeon to stay safely out of reach. As it was, she didn't want to strain the relationship between herself and Maya. Also, she didn't want to pay another emergency vet bill for a pigeon she didn't even own.

On the way over, they stopped to have lemonade at Esther's house — seated on the porch instead of inside with all the cats. Pirate plastered himself to the window, chattering every time Toes cooed.

Esther pushed the plate of muffins toward Maya. "Are you teaching class this week, or do you need more time to recover?"

For just a second, Maya and Toes had identical stares of confusion. "What?"

"Well, we assumed you would take over where JP left off. But I guess if you're not comfortable with that..." Esther trailed off in a way that made it clear she had expectations.

"Oh. But that was JP's... I mean, I guess if people want me to teach those classes... Are you sure people will want me to?"

"My dear, we would like nothing else. Good. That's settled. We'll see you tomorrow evening." She broke off a piece of muffin and offered it to Toes. "What a stylish bird."

"We're on our way to release him." Penelope finished her drink. "Want to come along?"

"I can't. The mahjong players will be here any minute now." She eyed Maya with a speculative look. "I don't suppose you play?"

"No. I designed a set of tile holders in ceramics class, but that's it." The corners of her mouth turned up. "My vases kept collapsing, and the teacups shattered in the kiln. The tile holders were the closest I could get to making something useful, since they wouldn't let us make bongs. I just barely passed the class."

Esther patted Maya's hand. "You're welcome to join the game if you want to learn. It's a lot of fun and new players are always welcome."

Penelope waited until she and Maya were two houses away before she said, "Don't let Esther's nice old lady act fool you. That group plays for money, and they'll fleece anyone who's just learning." Then she qualified her words. "I only lost ten dollars that afternoon, and most of that was to pay for pizza. I guess that's not that bad."

"If JP really did inherit all that money, I can probably afford it." Maya checked on Toes. "I have a hard time believing it's real."

"Probably best to keep some of that skepticism until the money's in your bank account."

"Yeah."

When they reached the house and the rental car wasn't in the driveway, they both gave a sigh of relief. "I knew he wasn't supposed to be here," Penelope said, "but you never know."

Ignoring the main house, they walked along the path to the backyard. Someone had removed the crime scene tape from the studio. Maya brightened. "I can go back inside? I'd love to grab some supplies, if you don't mind. After we release Toes."

"Fine by me," Penelope replied, while planning to make sure the loft doors were open if she needed to go inside.

When Maya put the carrier down and opened the door, Toes cooed and went back to eating the muffin. Maya gently tilted the carrier, but the pigeon moved further away from the opening. "Come on, Toes."

"He'll come out on his own when he's ready," Penelope said. "In the meantime, let's get what you need from the studio."

As Maya rolled open the unlocked door, she said, "After that whole carbon monoxide thing... Let me just open the shutters upstairs."

The idea of an unfinished second floor approachable only by ladder, with a gigantic hole in the floor, sang its siren song. Penelope dropped her backpack on the couch. "Can I come up, too?"

Maya nodded. "Just be careful on the ladder. I think the same guy who installed the water heater must have put that in, too."

The ladder was indeed a disaster waiting to happen, the wood of the rungs creaking and uneven. Penelope eased her way up, careful to distribute her weight across as much area as possible, and climbed onto the thankfully more solid loft floor. The view was breathtaking, though that might have been because once the hayloft doors were open, there was nothing to stop anyone from tumbling out. Penelope leaned forward to look straight down. From this angle, she couldn't tell if Toes had come out of the carrier yet. "They should build a slide from here."

"Down to a pool. We could make it a water slide." Maya considered the ground. "Might want to fix that ladder first, though."

Movement near the house made Penelope draw back into the shadows. There was Ricky Nash, irritably pushing a branch overhanging the path out of his way. She lowered her voice. "I thought you said he went to the capital?"

"What?" Maya's gaze followed Penelope's pointing finger. "What is he *doing* here?" She tiptoed to the corner of the loft over the front door and whispered, "Maybe if we keep quiet, he won't notice we're here."

Penelope joined her, feeling vaguely ridiculous, but hoping they could avoid an encounter with the man. "Maybe he's just here to pick up some paintings for an exhibition." That would be quick and he wouldn't notice they were up there.

"No. I always package them up for him." Maya leaned forward to peek over the loft edge. "Once I'm *really* done, I add the signature, give them a title, and then send them off to Ricky. Except for the ones JP gave to his friends. He had a habit of swiping them before I was done."

The hinges on the door beneath them squeaked, and Maya and Penelope fell silent. From where she stood, Penelope could see her backpack on the sofa. Surely, Ricky wouldn't notice it. And if he did, he'd assume she'd left it there when rescuing Maya from the carbon monoxide.

Down below, Ricky wandered around, flipping through the canvases stacked against the walls. Maya made a "hurry it up" gesture at him with one hand and sighed without making a sound. She leaned over to whisper into Penelope's ear. "He knows I hate it when he looks at them before they're finished."

Ricky hummed a cheerful tune and carried a canvas over to the easel. From the hayloft, Penelope couldn't see his face, but she watched him pick a clean brush from the mug and squeeze out a blob of black paint onto a scrap of paper. Carefully, he made a series of tiny brush strokes near the bottom right corner. Then he stood up, made one change, and swapped the canvas for another one.

Comprehension dawned on Maya's face. "That... snake!" Her whisper was lost in Ricky's humming. "I wasn't done with those!"

Maya might have been focused on the art, but Penelope noticed Ricky seemed very practiced at forging the Jean-Philippe Blanchet signature. How many times had he done this before? And how many of *those* paintings had he kept all the profits on, instead of the percentage afforded to him by the contract? If she was right, Ricky might have stolen tens of thousands — or more — from his clients.

Penelope decided to wait until Ricky had left to point that out to Maya. Ricky's humming could only drown out so many exclamations. Unfortunately, her phone was in her backpack on the sofa, so she couldn't even text Jake with the news or document Ricky's perfidy.

The door opened again, the rollers making a higher pitch as if someone had thrown the door open. Ricky's paintbrush clattered to the floor. Then he took a hesitant step forward. "Althea? What are you doing here?"

"Funny, I was about to ask you the same thing." Althea's husky voice held carefully controlled anger. She stalked forward, and Penelope shrank back against the wall, hoping Ricky's wife didn't turn around and look up. "Where is she?"

"Who?"

"Do you think I'm stupid?" Althea squared off against her husband. "Do you think I don't know why the 'assistant' always has to come along on all those trips?"

Maya turned to Penelope with a horrified look and shook her head. She mouthed, "No way!"

Penelope held a finger in front of her own lips. Getting caught by Ricky would have been bad enough; having Althea find the two of them right after accusing her husband of infidelity was bad on a whole other level. She wondered if she could jump out the hayloft window without breaking any bones. All those people in the parkour videos made it look so simple.

Down below, Althea patted the scrap of paper with the black paint and held up two fingers. "The paint is still *wet*, Ricky. Did she sneak past me into the house?"

"Althea, darling, you've entirely misunderstood the situation. When poor Jean-Philippe died, he left some of his work unfinished. And I thought... Who would it hurt if I added his signature to these paintings? Without a signature, they aren't worth anything, but signed..."

Wait. That sounded like Althea didn't know Maya was the artist behind Jean-Philippe Blanchet. Penelope mouthed, "He didn't tell his wife about you and JP?"

Maya shook her head. "NDA," she whispered back.

That was... interesting. More than interesting, Penelope realized. Because if Althea thought Maya was having an affair with her husband, she had a motive to kill Maya. And she was unaware that Maya's death would bring the income stream from Jean-Philippe Blanchet's paintings to an end. Althea had been in town with Ricky before JP was poisoned.

Means, motive, *and* opportunity — Althea had it all.

Penelope nearly vibrated with her need to talk to Jake about her new theory. The second Ricky and Althea left, she was going to call him. But first, they had to stay hidden.

Althea cut off her husband's rambling. "Where are you going?"

"Sweetie, let's just go to the capital like we'd planned." He must have been moving toward the door, because his voice came from beneath Penelope.

"She's around here somewhere, isn't she? That's why you're trying to get me to leave." After a moment, Althea spoke again, her voice icy. "Sit down."

Ricky's voice took on a panicked note. "Althea, honey, please don't point that at me."

Penelope and Maya stared at each other. Slowly shifting her weight forward, Penelope peeked through the loft opening. In the bright light of the studio, Althea's tiny silver gun gleamed.

Penelope eased back again. They were *definitely* waiting until Ricky and Althea left before going down the ladder.

Maya sneezed.

TWENTY-EIGHT

Maya had tried to muffle the sneeze in the crook of her elbow, but in the open room, there was no hiding it. Penelope winced.

Ricky and Althea broke off their argument and moved to the center of the room so they could look up at the loft. "Is someone up there?" Ricky asked.

Maya sneezed again.

Althea squinted toward the women. "It's *her*! I *knew* it!" She looked at her husband. "Sit down on the couch and don't make a move." Then she put the gun in the waist of her slacks and climbed up the ladder, stomping each rung in righteous fury. When her head popped above the floor and she saw Penelope, her anger turned to confusion. "Why are *you* here?"

"Me? I came here to help let the pigeon go."

Althea blinked.

Penelope decided now wasn't the time to explain. "Anyhow, it's been nice to see you, but it sounds like you and your husband have some things to discuss, so Maya and I are just going to go now." If they could just get out of the building, they would be safe. She walked toward the ladder confidently, as if expecting Althea to move out of the way.

Althea didn't move. Instead, she narrowed her eyes and looked between Penelope and Maya. "I think it's time for both of you to come down here so we can have a little chat."

Penelope considered whether it would be better to take her chances jumping out the loft door or try to talk her way out of this. All those kids with their parkour rolling could dive out head first with no consequences. But if *she* had to jump from the second floor, she would want to hang onto the edge and drop, which would take too much time. Better to go down the ladder and try to talk some sense into Althea. The other murder attempts had been staged to look like accidents — if Althea really was the killer, she wouldn't want to shoot the three of them.

As she followed Althea down to the ground, the ladder wobbled more than it had on the way up. Shoddy workmanship was the least of her problems at the moment, but it still made Penelope shake her head. How hard could it be to build and attach a sturdy ladder to this building which had been standing over a century? When she reached the bottom, she held the unstable side rail in place so Maya could make it safely down, and then they both joined Ricky on the couch.

Althea paced in front of the them, occasionally giving sharp glances to Maya and Ricky. She held the gun pointed at the floor, with her finger out of the trigger guard, so it looked like she knew something about how to handle guns. That could be good or bad. It made Althea less likely to accidentally shoot someone, but probably meant she'd spent time at the range improving her accuracy.

On Penelope's left, Maya seemed more confused than worried — Penelope was fairly certain Maya hadn't made the connection between Althea and JP's death, and it would be safer for all of them if it stayed that way for a while. Ricky, on Penelope's right, kept making moves as if he was going to stand up, only to subside when Althea glared at him.

Sometimes, the truth helped. Penelope kept her hands still on her lap. "Althea, your husband has been keeping secrets from you, but he's not having an affair with Maya."

Ricky turned to her with a haughty look. "I'll thank you for staying out of my private life."

Gesturing at the couch and then to Althea holding a gun by her side, Penelope said, "I'd *love* to stay out of your private life. But since that's the reason I'm stuck here instead of trying to find a mattress Jake and I can agree on, I'm in the middle of it."

Maya cocked her head. "Your guest bedroom mattress is pretty comfortable. You should just get another one of those."

"Right? I think so, too. But my husband wants something soft and I want something firm. I may just have to go with what he wants so we can get rid of the one we have. It's so lumpy, even Brutus has a hard time getting comfortable. The sales guy was trying to sell us one of those expensive ones you can set the dial on each side for what you want, but I'm not getting a mattress that spies on you." Penelope realized she was babbling, but couldn't stop herself.

Maya held up her index finger. "You know, you can get a firm mattress and then put a soft topper on half of it. That's what my aunt and uncle did."

"Really?" Distracted by this simple solution, Penelope shifted to face Maya. "Why wouldn't the mattress guy tell us that?" Then she rolled her eyes. "Of course. He's working on commission. Thank you. That may solve our problems."

When she faced forward again, Althea was staring at her in disbelief. "Sorry. It's just that we've been trying to decide which one to buy for so long..." She trailed off when Althea's expression didn't change. "Sorry."

"What did you mean Ricky is keeping secrets from me?"

Penelope tilted her head toward Maya. "She's the talent behind Jean-Philippe Blanchet. JP was just the public face."

"What?"

At the same time, Ricky said, "Nonsense. Darling, this woman is delusional. Let's just go. Maybe we could get a couple's massage after I drop these paintings off."

Maya shook her head and spoke to the ceiling. "He is *such* a liar. JP and I never should have signed that contract."

Althea stopped pacing and looked at her husband. "Is this true?"

"Of course not!"

Penelope added, "JP wasn't even French. His real name was John Phillips. He grew up in Scranton."

Althea stared wordlessly at Ricky, who didn't meet her eyes.

After a long moment, Althea said slowly, "Why wouldn't you tell me this?"

Ricky visibly changed course. "Sweetheart, you're the publicist. If you knew, you would have to lie, and that would make your work harder. This way, you believed everything you said."

Penelope and Maya shared a look. Ricky really *would* say anything to get out of trouble. The real reason likely had more to do with keeping damaging information from being used against him if his wife caught him cheating. Still, if this let them get out of there alive, she was willing to let him have his hypocrisy.

Penelope leaned forward. "So, you see, your husband

had to invite Maya along on every trip or someone would notice Jean-Philippe wasn't producing art in the place he was staying. It's all just a big misunderstanding."

"I guess." Althea considered that for a moment in silence.

Penelope grabbed her backpack. As soon as she and Maya were back to the street, she was calling Jake to tell him everything. The police could deal with Althea and her homicidal tendencies. "Okay. So, we're going to go—"

Althea cut her off. "If *she*," Althea waved her gun at Maya, causing both Penelope and Maya to lean back, "is the artist, why are *you*," and this time she leveled the gun at her husband, leaving it just a bit longer, "forging the signatures?"

"Because he's a snake," Maya said with some heat.

"Snakes aren't really that bad," Penelope noted. "They're actually kind of nice."

Maya nodded, granting her that point. "You're right. Snakes are too good for him." She leaned over to look at Ricky. "You were just going to take those and keep the entire sale, weren't you?"

"Of course not."

At least Maya hadn't yet realized this wasn't the first time, or she would be even angrier.

Maya grabbed the cushion behind her with both hands and reached past Penelope to whack Ricky's face. "You're been stealing from us the whole time, haven't you? Those missing paintings never show up on the books. I didn't believe JP when he said he hadn't taken them, and it was you all along!"

No, apparently Maya *had* figured it out. Penelope pushed against the back of the couch to avoid the pillow fight happening in front of her.

Althea sauntered closer to her husband, looking even

more dangerous. "Ricky darling." Her voice was sickly sweet. "If you've been stealing from your artists, where has that money been going? It's not going into our bank account. I check that against the receipts."

"It... It..." Ricky's Adam's apple bobbed as he stared at his wife.

"I can forgive your infidelity as long as I know it won't happen again, but I can't abide you stealing from me," Althea purred.

Maya clutched the couch cushion to her chest. "It was *you* trying to kill me!"

Unable to stop herself, Penelope rubbed the spot between her eyes where a headache threatened. Their best chance of getting out alive had been convincing Althea they didn't suspect her. That ship had now sailed.

Meanwhile, Ricky had found his words again. "Darling, I didn't *steal* from you. I was keeping it for unexpected expenses."

Once again, Althea looked uncertain, but Penelope didn't care if Ricky talked his way out of this. Althea knew Maya and Penelope had figured out she was the one who had killed JP. Now Althea had a motive to kill *them*.

Easing her hand into her backpack while Althea was distracted, Penelope found her phone and typed the sequence to unlock it. Or at least, she tried to. With no buttons, she was guessing at her finger placement, but she'd done this so many times her fingers had to know the way. The phone app was on the lower left, and then the favorites screen was... the icon on the left? Or the one right next to it? She tapped a space on the left, though she had no idea if she was even close to the row of icons. Still unable to look at the screen, she tapped near the top.

If she had unlocked her phone, and *if* she had opened

the phone app, and *if* she had reached the favorites list, she'd either dialed Jake or Esther. But there was no way to tell without looking. But maybe she could glance down long enough to text for help...

The rumble of a motorcycle pulling to a stop in front of the house distracted Althea from her musings. She straightened with a start and saw Penelope's hand in her backpack. "Give me that!" Ripping it from Penelope's lap, she tossed it in the corner.

Penelope gritted her teeth. Her chance of that call going through and alerting someone in time was nearly zero. She'd have to figure out some other way out of this mess.

When footsteps sounded on the path coming up to the studio, Althea trained her gun on the three of them and tiptoed to stand next to the door.

Lilac's voice came from outside. "Ricky? Are you here?"

Ricky made a quiet noise of anguish. Penelope turned her head to look at him. "Really?" she whispered. "You and *Lilac*?"

"Huh." Maya pushed the couch cushion behind her. "I did *not* see that coming."

"It's *business*," Ricky hissed.

"Yeah, right," Maya whispered back.

The door slid open. "Do you need help boxing..." Lilac trailed off as she saw Althea. "I guess Ricky finally told you, then."

Ricky whimpered. Penelope blew out a long breath. They were definitely going to need to rescue themselves.

Toes fluttered down from the loft to land in Maya's lap, cooing softly.

Once again, Althea's tone was icy. "Told me what?"

Lilac's voice carried the disdain that only someone young, beautiful, and wealthy could pull off. "Althea. You had your run. Don't embarrass yourself by trying to hold on to what you can't have. With Ricky's connections in the art world, and mine in society, we'll be able to do things you never could." Then she noticed the gun in Althea's hand and drew back uncertainly. "That's not real, is it?"

With a bang, a chunk of wood from the door jamb went flying. Althea gestured with the still-smoking gun. "Get over there with the rest of them."

Suddenly pale, Lilac scurried across the room to stand behind Ricky.

"I'm team nobody," Maya muttered, stroking Toes's feathers.

Penelope was torn. Normally, she would have supported without hesitation any woman whose husband had taken up with a younger version of herself. But Penelope was making an exception in this case. "Me, too."

If only she'd brought Brutus along. Without Penelope keeping him in check, he might have knocked over Althea while trying to be her friend. But no, Althea might have shot the mastiff. It was good Brutus was at home. And Jake might have known how to overpower Althea, but Penelope didn't want anyone pointing a gun at him ever again.

"This is bad," Maya whispered, as Lilac and Althea argued over Ricky's head.

Penelope silently agreed. So what did she have to work with? Her phone was in her backpack, *maybe* connected to someone who would send help, but she couldn't reach it to check.

Toes cooed, completely unconcerned by the tension in the room.

Hold on. Althea was deathly afraid of birds. All they needed was enough of a distraction so they could run past Althea and get outside without being shot. "Get ready to run," Penelope whispered to Maya. She reached over and scooped up Toes.

The pigeon settled in her cupped hands, content to look around the room. With Althea between her and the door, Penelope needed to plan this so the woman with the gun went to the left, opening up a path. She leaned forward and tossed Toes toward Althea's left ear.

Toes played his part perfectly, as if they'd practiced this trick before. He flapped his wings and tried to land on Althea's head, causing her to shriek, duck, and flail at the pigeon, the gun in her hand completely forgotten. Penelope jumped to her feet.

But Althea's panicked moves had taken her in the wrong direction, and she stumbled back into the door, still yelling as she batted at her hair. Penelope changed direction, sprinting for the ladder to the loft, Toes flying up ahead of her.

"Stop!" Althea yelled.

Penelope ignored her, scrambling up the wobbling rungs. A shot rang out. She flinched, but kept going. Most people, even trained law enforcement officers, missed most of their targets in live action, and if Penelope didn't get out and find help, four people might die.

Four more rungs and she would reach the loft. Althea wouldn't be able to see her there, and Penelope could make it out the loft door.

Wood cracked. The rung she had just grabbed came off in her hand. Then, the left side rail of the ladder fell backward. Time slowed. As the entire structure disintegrated, she realized the rungs were held on with two nails pounded through the side rail into the wood of the rung. Her first thought was *No wonder the whole thing was so unstable.* Close on its heels was *When did Red and Sons renovate barns?* Because there was no way this had been constructed by anyone else.

Penelope clutched the right side rail as the rest of the rungs clattered to the ground. For a moment, she thought she'd be able to shimmy up the two-by-four she was holding, but then it, too, slowly tilted backward.

Penelope dropped to the ground, just barely getting her legs under her. Her momentum was too great to remain standing, and she ended up on her rear with pieces of broken lumber all around her.

Althea stood a few feet away, shaking her head, still holding her gun.

Penelope let the rail in her hand fall to the ground with a clatter. "Oops."

TWENTY-NINE

Back on the couch next to Maya, Penelope shrugged. "We tried." It was easier to ignore her bruised tailbone when she looked at the gun Althea held. "Toes went out the loft door."

"Oh, good." Maya sagged back, and as she did so, something hard poked Penelope in the leg. She glanced down to see a phone sticking up from the gap in the cushions. Maya raised her eyebrows and whispered, "Lean forward a little."

Clever. While Penelope had tried an alternate escape route when Althea blocked the door, Maya had taken the opportunity to grab her phone. Penelope sat forward just enough for Maya to hold the phone behind her back.

After a moment, Maya moved her hands to her lap and nodded once. "I sent a text."

Penelope sat back, feeling the phone behind her. They'd done everything they could. Now they just had to stay alive and wait for help.

Meanwhile, Althea had gone back to pacing, and Ricky tried to appease his wife. "Darling, I love you. You know that. We can get through this."

Lilac crossed her arms, somehow still looking like a

high-fashion model while doing so, and shifted her weight so she moved away from Ricky. "You're such a pig."

With a snort, Maya said, "Pigs are too good for him, too. Everything's too good for him."

Ricky turned to glare at Maya. "You're not helping!"

"*I'm* not helping. Your wife has tried to kill me — twice! — because you were unfaithful. You got us into this mess." Maya considered for a moment. "And you've been stealing from me and JP this whole time." She twisted to look at Lilac. "Don't trust this guy."

Althea seemed to come to some conclusion. She stopped pacing and looked around the studio. "Ah. That will do nicely." Picking up the can of turpentine from Maya's worktable, she carried it over to the door, where dozens of canvases leaned against the walls. With a glance toward her captives to make sure nobody had moved, she crouched down, set her gun on the ground, and unscrewed the lid of the can. The pungent odor of turpentine filled the room. Leaving the turpentine uncapped, she grabbed the gun and unplugged a floor lamp before dragging it to the same spot.

"What does she think she's doing?" Maya asked in a low voice. "If she gets turpentine on those paintings, she'll destroy them."

That made Ricky sit forward. "Althea, darling, I know you're mad at me, but damaging the art only hurts both of us."

Althea had opened a pocketknife and was stripping the insulation from the lamp cord. Now she looked up and smiled sweetly. "Don't fret, Ricky. You won't have to worry about a thing."

Lilac hissed at Ricky, "Those are *our* paintings. Do something!"

Maya turned around, offense in every line of her posture. "What do you mean, they're *your* paintings? *I'm* the one who painted them."

Ricky dropped his head into his hands.

Lilac frowned. "What are you talking about?"

Althea laughed from across the room, where she was still working on the cord. "There's one thing about Ricky that you can always count on. He lies to *everyone*. It turns out JP was just a pretty face and Maya was doing all the work."

Lilac turned to Ricky. "What?"

His chin jutted out. "Oh, please, as if I was going to tell you that. You'd just spent months trying to lure JP away to start some ridiculous artists' colony."

"We were talking about getting married and opening an agency together, and now I find that you didn't trust me at all!"

They glared at each other.

Across the room, Althea's hands stilled as she regarded her husband. "Hiring someone to be the public face of an artist is actually a stroke of genius. It's *almost* enough to make me forget about your affairs."

Ricky popped to his feet. "I have more ideas. Let's sit down over a nice lunch and talk them over." He froze as Althea dropped her pocketknife and picked up the gun.

"I said *almost*," Althea growled. She waited for him to sit again before she continued working on the cord. A few seconds later, she nodded in satisfaction. "There. That should work." Standing, she looked around the studio. "Now, what am I forgetting?"

Althea acted like someone who was planning to leave and not worry about anyone following her, which worried Penelope. "The police will be here soon, Althea. You might as well close up the turpentine and have a seat. There's no point in ruining the paintings."

"Oh, right, the paintings. That's what it was." Althea walked over to the second easel. "Now which ones did Ricky sign... Ah, these two. Thanks for reminding me." She opened the studio door and set the paintings outside. Then she came back inside and plugged in the lamp. "The trouble with art supplies is that so many of them are flammable."

With the toe of one stylish shoe, Althea knocked over the open can of turpentine. The contents pooled in front of the door, and the odor got stronger. If the loft doors had been closed, it would have been impossible to breathe. She flipped on the lamp.

Nothing happened. Penelope wasn't surprised, having been involved in far too many of her son's science fair projects. Nothing ever worked on the first try.

Althea shrugged. "It only has to look plausible." She switched the gun to her left hand and took a lighter from her pocket. With a quick gesture, she lit the edge of the turpentine and stepped outside, rolling the door closed behind her.

Thick smoke rose from the burning turpentine, filling the room and curling up into the loft. "The paintings!" Ricky cried. He dashed over to pull the canvases away from the fire, then doubled over, coughing. Lilac took the canvases and dragged them farther away.

Penelope held her breath and tried to open the door, but Althea had propped something against it from the outside. Though Penelope thought she might be able to break it open, the effort would involve standing in the pool of burning turpentine. She retreated and looked around the room.

The ground floor windows had been painted shut. The

only other way out of the building was through the loft doors, but the ladder had fallen apart and there was no way to get up there.

Or was there?

From under the worktable, Maya gave a shout of triumph and held up a tiny fire extinguisher. "Found it!" She moved forward, spraying the base of the fire. The flames decreased, but leapt up again as the turpentine reignited. Crouching to avoid the smoke, Maya kept spraying.

They couldn't stay there and hope the extinguisher would take care of the flames. Penelope dragged the couch to the remains of the ladder, then heaved it up onto its end, leaning it against the wall. Standing on a wobbly chair, she climbed onto the arm of the sofa and stood. That put the floor of the loft at waist height. She jumped and flopped onto the loft floor with all the grace of a walrus on land, but the air was a little clearer.

"Dang it!" Maya yelled from below. "This isn't working!" She coughed.

No time for finesse. In a gap between the houses, Penelope saw the Nashes's red convertible speed off. Althea was getting away, but at least Penelope didn't have to worry about being shot. In the distance, sirens wailed. All the dogs in the neighborhood howled along.

Penelope sat with her feet out the loft door and shoved herself forward until she dropped.

In all the parkour videos she'd marveled over, they made falling from heights look like a simple matter of rolling to their feet afterward and running toward the next obstacle. Penelope's feet slipped on the gravel, causing her to thump down on her tailbone. "Ow," she said proactively, not waiting for the pain to start. Perhaps her jump hadn't been graceful, but she was on the ground. Scrambling to her feet, she ran around to the front of the studio and kicked away the shovel Althea had used to wedge the door closed.

Thick black smoke poured through the gap as Penelope slid open the door. "Maya?"

Maya stumbled out, still coughing, followed by Lilac, who somehow looked like she was on a catwalk ignoring a malfunctioning fog machine. After a three-second gap, while Penelope was psyching herself up to run inside to find Ricky, he staggered out, a stack of canvases held under both arms.

Toes flapped over the fence from the yard next door and landed on Maya's shoulder, just as the first firefighters ran around the house and Jake sprinted past them. He saw his wife and nearly tripped in relief.

Penelope leaned into her husband's embrace. "I knew you'd show up."

THIRTY

As more firefighters appeared, Penelope let Jake walk her away from the building.

"Are you okay?"

"My butt's a little sore." Penelope raised her head. "I got to jump out the hayloft doors. Just like in all those videos." She remembered her descent to the ground. "Except maybe not quite as graceful. I need more practice."

Jake lifted his face to the sky, closed his eyes, and shook his head. In the building, larger fire extinguishers whooshed. The column of smoke abated quickly as the firefighters pushed the nearly empty can of turpentine outside and smothered the flames indoors. Paramedics crouched around Ricky, who was sitting on the ground with a stack of canvases clutched to his chest.

Lilac tossed her hair back and stared daggers at her would-be business partner.

As Penelope wiped her streaming eyes on the hem of her shirt, she realized she'd flashed half the first responders in the city. "We need to find Detective Sanchez. Althea killed JP while she was trying to kill Maya. And she just tried to murder the four of us."

"Brianna's on her way."

"Oh, oh, oh!" Penelope jumped up and down in excitement. "And I know how to solve our mattress problem!"

THIRTY-ONE

It took less than a day before Althea was arrested and charged with attempted murder for the fire she'd set, with more murder and attempted murder charges expected soon.

"I can't believe she thought I'd have an affair with Ricky," Maya said as she and Penelope carried the smoke-damaged sofa out of the studio. "Ricky, of all people!"

Since Maya had decided to stay in town, at least until the end of the original residency, they were making the studio usable again. Everything that couldn't be wiped down or painted over needed to go. To be fair, almost every stick of furniture in the studio had needed to be thrown out even *before* the fire.

Esther, in her capacity as Rose Garden Society organizer, had convinced the landlord to have a dumpster delivered, but Maya had turned down the offer to have a cleaning crew take over, because she was worried they would use toxic products that might harm Toes.

"Althea suspected Ricky was having an affair with *someone*, and you kept avoiding her, so she assumed it was because you had a guilty conscience." Penelope backed up the ramp into the rented dumpster and they dropped the sofa in the corner. Pushing an errant strand of hair behind her ear, she followed Maya back into the studio.

"I avoid almost everyone," the artist argued. "That's not proof of anything. What do you think about this?" She nudged a padded armchair with her foot. "I could probably throw out the cushions and recover it."

Penelope watched a sprinkle of sawdust float to the floor. "I think it's infested with something and you should get rid of it. If you want a replacement, I can take you to the thrift store." Then she remembered Maya was inheriting JP's family money. "Or we could probably find something at the antique stores if you don't mind the cost."

Maya blinked. "I guess I could afford it now." She shook her head. "I'd feel bad getting paint on a valuable antique."

They carried the armchair out to the dumpster and tossed it on the couch. "The only thing I don't understand," Penelope said as she brushed sawdust off her hands, "is how Althea could have thought you wouldn't smell the poison hemlock in the smoothie. JP obviously wouldn't have smelled it because he couldn't smell anything. But you would have unscrewed the lid and stopped. I got a whiff of it — nobody who had a sense of smell could have accidentally drunk it."

"I'm not completely sure," Maya admitted. "But every time Althea is around, my nose gets all stuffed up. I think I'm allergic to something in her perfume. She might have thought my sinuses were always clogged."

There was something satisfying about Althea's perfume being her downfall.

On the way back to the studio, Maya stopped to look at

the bedraggled yard where the bushes showed signs of being trampled by firefighters' boots. Then she looked further to the dilapidated house beyond. "Is it weird that I still like it here?" She'd moved her things back into the house earlier that morning.

Penelope stopped next to her. "You're welcome to stay at our house as long as you want. There's no rush."

"I know. Thanks. But I miss being able to walk across the yard to the studio whenever I want. And I was thinking last night — maybe I'll just keep renting this house even after the residency is over. Then I wouldn't have to move again, and this seems like a nice place." She waved her hand. "You know. Now that Althea isn't trying to kill me."

As much as Penelope wanted Maya to stay, there were practical issues. "Ricky isn't going to keep showing up?"

"Ricky," Maya said darkly, "has agreed to tear up our contract and never talk to me again as long as I don't press charges against him for stealing the paintings. So I officially own the Jean-Philippe Blanchet name and I can paint whatever I want." She followed Penelope into the studio.

"Good." Picking up a pile of splintered two by fours leftover from the poorly constructed ladder, Penelope added, "Though it seems unfair that he's going to get away scot free."

"Well..." Maya picked up the smoke-damaged cushions and they went outside. "I'm no longer bound by the NDA. And what are the chances that Ricky did this to me and JP and not to any of his other clients?" She spun the cushions into the dumpster one by one. "That was what that letter from Sheehan and Pitt was about. Sheehan called this morning after he heard about JP's death."

"Oh?"

"When JP realized he was going to inherit his grandfather's money, he talked to Sheehan about investigating Ricky's business, to try to find some way out of our contract. JP didn't tell me about it, so I wouldn't be involved if it all went wrong."

"JP wasn't a bad guy." Penelope looked around the room. "We've got all the big stuff out. Let's move everything over. We can start wiping down the walls on that side." The smoke had left a residue that would need to be removed before the walls were repainted. Outside, a car's tires crunched on the path going to the studio. Jake had arrived. "And did Sheehan find anything?"

"I think so. He started to explain it all, but I got lost. I *hate* talking on the phone." She and Penelope crab-walked the work table to the other side of the room. "He's flying out here to explain it to me in person."

Lawyers did nothing for free, and JP hadn't yet collected money from his inheritance when he'd talked to Sheehan. So where had the money for the retainer come from? One second after Penelope thought about it, she had the answer. "JP gave him a painting as payment."

"Yeah. JP asked me to paint something for a friend of his a few months ago. I think that must have been it."

Not giving Ricky his cut of the painting was certainly against their contract, but Penelope thought Ricky would be too busy with his upcoming legal problems to go after JP's estate.

Jake walked in with an aluminum ladder held in one hand and a bucket of tools in the other, and Penelope took a moment to admire his casual competence. No matter what was needed, her husband always helped without complaining. If he didn't have the knowledge or skills to do something, he either learned it on his own or found someone who could teach him.

Now he grinned at her. "Come hold the ladder while I strap it in place."

Penelope refused to feel embarrassed for getting caught checking out her husband. "Anything you need."

THIRTY-TWO

Later that evening, Penelope lounged on the couch in their living room, with her laptop in front of her and Brutus snoring at her feet. Her back rested on Jake's shoulder. On the television, players swept their brooms madly on the ice.

"Do you think I could learn to do that?" She gestured at the video playing on her screen, which showed a series of young people somersaulting off a roof and landing unharmed on the pavement below.

"Yes, but I might have a heart attack while watching you."

"We could learn together." Penelope imagined the video with the two of them in place of the teenagers. Obviously, they couldn't wear the same clothes without looking foolish, but they had their own style.

Jake brought his arm around her and kissed the top of her head. "Last week, I hurt my big toe while sleeping. Our parkour days may be behind us."

"You're probably right," Penelope conceded. "It looks fun, though."

"Maybe we could take up curling instead," he suggested.

They watched as a player swung the stone and knelt while sliding across the ice. The whole process was controlled and graceful.

"We would have to move somewhere with an ice rink. And I'm not great with a broom."

Jake coughed and stayed silent.

Penelope tipped her head back and smiled at him. "Such restraint." After being married to one man who thought it was her job to do all the housework, Penelope had made it very clear to Jake when they first started dating that she expected a partner, not a supervisor.

"I may be slow sometimes, but I'm not going to fall for that." He settled back to watch the screen. "I'm not sure this is your sport, though. You thought golf was too repetitious."

Jake knew her well. Watching people slide across the ice and hearing the crowd react was fine, but if she had to practice the same moves over and over again, she would be testing her ability to perform a pirouette on ice in less than ten minutes. "That's why parkour would be a much better fit."

"When's the last time you did a somersault?"

"Probably Seth's mommy-and-me gymnastics class when he was a toddler." Had it really been thirty years? She still felt the same. Better, in many ways.

"Okay. We'll go in the backyard tomorrow, and if you can do five somersaults and you still want to learn parkour, we'll sign up for the next class at the expensive gym."

"Deal." Penelope closed her laptop and snuggled into him. "But if the new mattress hurts my back, I want a raincheck." They'd taken Maya's advice and purchased a firm mattress with a soft topper that covered one side, and it had been delivered earlier in the day. Brutus had spent the afternoon sleeping on it.

"The new mattress is too expensive to hurt your back." Jake's voice was firm.

"Is that how it works?"

"Yes."

"Huh." Penelope waited until the players finished the end. "We really should try it out."

"Curling?"

A laugh escaped her. "No. The mattress."

"Ah." Jake hit the button on the remote and the television went dark. "I like this plan."

"I thought you might." She let him help her to her feet, and they went up the stairs together.

ACKNOWLEDGMENTS

Here we are again, in the part of the book where I admit that getting this novel into your hands isn't just a matter of lounging on the couch in solitary splendor while filling three notebooks with perfectly formed cursive using my expensive fountain pen.

Everything about that is, of course, correct, aside from the lounging on the couch (which is the dog's place), the notebooks (sorry, it's all on a computer), the expensive fountain pen (which my foster kittens would take and destroy), and the perfectly formed cursive.

(My first truly bad grade in school was for handwriting and — shockingly — this did not give my younger self any incentive to improve.)

But the biggest lie in that first paragraph is the "solitary" bit. Yes, I have written all the words, but I relied on a lot of people to get me to that point. So thank you to my writing group partners, both the ones who encourage me to sit down and put words on the (virtual) page, and those who see the book before it's ready for public consumption, offering advice on everything from the absence of crucial characters in the first half of the book, to the distressing lack of commas pretty much everywhere else.

(To be clear, the comma thing distresses Ana, not me. I've always taken a "if it's clear, it's good enough" approach to punctuation, which perhaps explains some of my English grades. Though I think that might also have been due to a quarter spent on diagramming sentences, a skill which, to this day, makes *absolutely* no sense to me. Who knows? Perhaps I'd be winning major literary awards if only I'd applied myself in sixth grade! But I doubt it.)

The rules say I also have to thank my brother Eric (I put no comma there on purpose, Ana, because I have two other brothers, whom I'm not thanking here because they didn't do anything helpful) who did the final proofreading. *He* probably understands how to diagram a sentence, but his usefulness here is more because he's willing to put in some real effort to tell me I did something wrong.

(Eric also left a note in the manuscript saying, "Pigeons are not quiet. If one starts cooing at 3:30 AM in front of your window, you'll understand." To which I say: Obviously, Eric has never owned a conure or even a cockatiel. Trust me on this.)

Finally, a big round of gratitude to everyone who has read the Penelope Standing series, told their friends about it, or left reviews. You are literally the reason this book exists at all. Thank you from the bottom of my heart!

ABOUT THE AUTHOR

Tess Baytree is the pen name of mystery and speculative fiction author Theresa Baumgartner. At various times she has been a veterinarian, Unix system administrator, software developer, and after-hours book-shelver in a medical library.

Theresa currently lives in Northern California in a house with too many animals. She knits hats for garden gnomes and runs with scissors only when absolutely necessary.

Want updates about new releases? Silly dog anecdotes? Join the newsletter mailing list! Go to https://tmbaumgartner.com/subscribe/ or point your phone's camera at the QR code above.

ALSO BY TESS BAYTREE

As Tess Baytree:

Death Walks a Dog (Penelope Standing #1)

Death Tracks the Scent (Penelope Standing #2)

Death Smells a Rose (Penelope Standing #3)

Death Trims the Tree (holiday novella)

Death Crashes a Wedding (Penelope Standing #4)

Death Paints a Picture (Penelope Standing #5)

As T.M. Baumgartner:

Shift Happens

The Chaos Job (Jackpot Drift #1)

The Chaos Connection (Jackpot Drift #2)

The Chaos Nexus (Jackpot Drift #3)

Dragon Freehold

All Gremlins Great & Small (The Portal Storms #0)

All Rocs Wise & Wonderful (The Portal Storms #1)

All Basilisks Wild & Sparking (The Portal Storms #2)

www.ingramcontent.com/pod-product-compliance
Lightning Source LLC
LaVergne TN
LVHW091139080826
845145LV00008B/2200